# ONE
# MOMENT
## IN
# TIME

## ALSO BY LAUREN BARNHOLDT

# ONE MOMENT IN TIME

### THE MOMENT OF TRUTH BOOK 2

## LAUREN BARNHOLDT

An Imprint of HarperCollinsPublishers

HarperTeen is an imprint of HarperCollins Publishers.

Library of Congress catalog card number: 2014959936
ISBN 978-0-06-232141-1 (pbk.)

Typography by Ellice M. Lee
15 16 17 18 19   CG/RRDH   10 9 8 7 6 5 4 3 2 1
❖
First Edition

FOR AARON, ALWAYS

# ONE

From: Quinn Reynolds (Quinn.Reynolds@brightonhillshigh.edu)
To: Quinn Reynolds (Quinn.Reynolds@brightonhillshigh.edu)

Before graduation, I promise to . . . *do something crazy*.

I've thought about that email once in a while, but it's not like I'm obsessed with it or anything. How could I be? *Before graduation, I promise to do something crazy?* What does that even mean? It's the kind of stupid thing you write when you're fourteen and have no idea what it is you're supposed to put in an email to your future self.

Besides, the whole idea of sending the emails in the first place was ridiculously childish. (I can't remember whose plan it was exactly, but it must have been Aven's, because there's no way it was mine or Lyla's—that kind of thing has Aven written all over it.)

Anyway, when the email arrives in my in-box on the morning of our senior trip to Florida, I read it, sigh, and then send it to my trash. I don't feel the need to do something crazy, now or ever. The craziest thing I've ever done is put blond highlights in my hair, and even then they were the kind that washed out in sixteen to eighteen shampoos. I didn't even go out and buy some cheap drugstore hair dye—I got them done properly, at the salon.

"This is so lame," my friend Celia says from where she's sitting next to me. We're on the bus that's going to take us from the school to the airport so we can catch our flight to Florida. She wrinkles her tiny, adorably freckled nose. "I hate school buses. They smell like vomit and old leather."

"They should have let us drive our own cars," my friend Paige says. She's sitting in the seat ahead of us, her back against the window, leaning forward just a little bit so that her shiny blond hair doesn't hit the glass. "Everyone knows school buses are, like, super dangerous." She picks at a piece of duct tape that's coming loose from the top of the seat. "And this one is falling apart."

Celia sighs, then taps her fingers against her purse impatiently. "I can't wait until we're relaxing on the beach." She motions me toward her, then puts a finger to her lips, like she's about to let me in on a secret. She opens her purse and gives me a peek at what's inside.

"Jesus, Celia," I say, pushing it away from me. "Are you

insane? You can't bring that on the plane."

"I'm not going to bring it on the *plane*," she says, rolling her eyes at me like I'm a complete idiot. "We'll smoke it in the bathroom before we board."

"That's a horrible idea," I say. "A completely horrible idea." I wonder why she's even telling me this. She knows I don't smoke pot. I don't like the feeling of being out of control. (Not that I know pot would make me feel out of control, since I've never smoked it. But I don't really want to find out.)

"She's right," Paige says. She reaches into her Louis Vuitton classic printed clutch and pulls out a pair of Gucci sunglasses, which she puts on even though we're still in Connecticut and the sun isn't even out. "We'll smoke it in the parking lot and then ditch it."

I take in a deep breath through my nose and let it out through my mouth, wondering how it is that I'm even friends with these girls when the three of us are so different.

Things I have in common with Celia and Paige:

1.  We are smart. Like, very smart. We take all AP classes and are still ranked one (me), two (Paige), and four (Celia) in our class. Viet Cho is number three, which has really put a crimp in our plans, since Celia got it in her head that if he wasn't, we could do something really fun, like wear T-shirts to graduation that say 1, 2, 3 on them or make

up songs with one, two, three in the lyrics. Which actually really wouldn't have worked, since everyone knows you wear a cap and gown to graduation. Although I guess some people wear crazy outfits underneath—like last year Duke Marrone wore a bikini under his cap and gown and everyone thought it was hilarious. Our parents would never let us do something like that, though. It would ruin their graduation-day pictures, the ones where they'll be standing there looking like perfect parents with their perfect daughters. Besides, if Celia is so concerned about us being numbers one, two, and three, then she should just work harder. She's naturally smart, but she doesn't really study that much. She could have easily been number three with just a little more effort.

2. We're all going to Ivy League colleges. Celia's going to Yale, Paige to Harvard, and me to Stanford. At least, I will be once I get in. You'd think I'd be upset we're all going to be in different cities, but I honestly don't really care. Paige and Celia are my high school friends, the kind of friends you're close with during high school and then end up sort of forgetting about after graduation. I'll hunt them down on Facebook in ten years and see pictures of them hanging out at the Yale Club with their lawyer husbands. (Although lawyers really don't make as much money as they used to, so I'm not sure if Celia and Paige will end up marrying lawyers. Maybe they'll

be married to investment bankers—by then the econ-
omy will hopefully be in another boom and investment
bankers will be the hot thing again.)

3.  We're all rich. I know it's awful to just blurt that out, but
    it's true. We're rich. Well, our parents are rich. Which
    I guess means that technically we're not rich, we just
    come from rich families.

The three of us pretend to be best friends, but really . . .
there's always been kind of a distance between us. It's not
anything to do with Paige and Celia. At least, I don't think
it is. The distance between us is the same distance I feel
between me and anyone, really. So maybe the problem isn't
Celia and Paige—maybe it's me.

"Show me your tattoo," Paige says to Celia, leaning farther over the seat.

Celia grins and reaches down, pushing the top of her
jeans over her hip bone. A tattoo of a tiny black butterfly
appears, the skin around the outline still raw.

"Does it hurt?" I ask.

"Not anymore," Celia says. "But it hurt like a bitch while
I was getting it done." She keeps the top of her jeans held
down, showing off her tattoo. I have to admit it is kind of
pretty. But what's it going to look like when she's seventy?
And seriously, a butterfly? It's so . . . I don't know, pedes-
trian. They probably have assistant tattoo artists giving

everyone butterflies, like how when you go to the doctor they have a physician's assistant to take care of run-of-the-mill concerns.

I really shouldn't be so judge-y.

I lean back in my seat and pull out my phone to check the time. 7:59 a.m. One minute until we head out. The informational packet they gave us made it very clear that the bus to the airport was going to leave at eight a.m., and not a minute after. It said no latecomers would be allowed, and that if you missed the bus, you were out of luck. Not that anyone was going to miss the bus. I mean, what kind of idiot is late for their senior trip?

I sigh and scroll through my emails, looking for anything important I may have missed. I applied for a summer internship in Palo Alto this summer, at a biotech company that specializes in doing research on gene-specific diseases. If I get the position, I know I'm not *really* going to be doing research—no one's going to let some seventeen-year-old kid near anything important. It's going to be a lot of getting people coffee and filing reports. But it's still pretty amazing.

My mom's friend knew someone who knew someone, and she was able to get me an interview. Actually, that's not completely true—she put me in touch with her contact person, but I set up the interview on my own. Biogene has offices in Palo Alto, Sarasota, Columbus, and Seattle. The woman in charge of the Palo Alto office hooked me up with her colleague in the Sarasota office, and so I've been playing email tag with her, trying to figure out a time for me to come down and meet her while I'm in Florida. Technically an in-person interview isn't required, but I figure a little face time can't hurt. It will give me an edge over the other candidates. I actually present very well in person. I think it's because I look so wholesome.

"Get off your phone," Celia demands, sounding annoyed. She snaps her jeans back into place and gathers her long hair into a ponytail. "We need to make plans for our trip."

"I'm just making sure I don't have an email from the Biogene woman," I say, still scrolling. No email. Wow. I replied to Margot's last email, like, yesterday morning. Either I'm at the bottom of the totem pole when it comes to things she has to think about, or that place is really not well run.

"You know you're going to get the internship," Paige says. "So who cares if you meet up with them?"

"Yeah," Celia says. "Cancel that shit. It's going to cut into our tanning time."

"I don't need any tanning time," I say. "I burn."

"You just need to wear sunscreen," Celia says, continuing her pattern of trying to insist she knows more about me than I know about myself. "I'll give you some. I have coconut-scented."

"Thanks," I say, because I don't want to get into it.

And that's when I see it.

The email.

To me.

From STANFORD ADMISSIONS.

My heart leapfrogs into my throat.

Stanford is the very last school I've been waiting to hear from. They've actually been late with their decision, because even though I double- and triple-checked my application like a million billion trillion times before sending it in, somehow it didn't end up arriving. One of those fluke things with servers and cyberspace, I guess. Luckily, my mom knew someone who knew someone in admissions (yeah, I know, my mom knows everyone—she's a doctor and my dad works in medical research, so they're pretty well connected), and they were able to figure out a way to let me send my application in after the deadline. But because of the delay, they've been late in getting back to me.

The only other schools I applied to were Georgetown, Brown, and Yale. I got into all three. But I have no interest in any of them. Not that they're not great schools, because they are. But Stanford is where I want to be. It's the only place I've *ever* wanted to be. It's where my parents went, it's where my brother goes, it's in California, where people are innovative and laid-back, where they eat wheatgrass shots and wear flip-flips to their jobs at hip-sounding new start-up companies. I'm going to be premed. And then I'm going to Stanford's medical school. You know, where Cristina Yang went. And yes, it's lame to want to go somewhere just because a fictional TV character went there, but come on—it's Cristina Yang. Stanford is the hub of gene research, where everyone is doing exciting things, where the sun is shining and . . . I just really, really want to go there.

I wait a moment before opening the email. It's this thing that I do sometimes, when something really good is about to happen. I take a second to enjoy the feeling. The brain is constantly making new neurons, constantly creating new connections, and the longer you savor certain feelings and moments, the stronger those connections become. You can actually become a happier person just by training your brain to make new pathways when you're happy.

I'm going to remember this moment forever. I'll tell my children all about it when *they* get into Stanford. I'll show them my college yearbook pictures, and they'll laugh at how ridiculous I look. But of course they'll still want to go to Stanford—they'll be smart enough to be able to look past my out-of-date fashion choices and see how amazing it is.

I take in a deep breath and open the email.

At that exact moment, the bus lurches into motion, and the words on the screen blur for a second before coming back into focus.

Dear Quinn,

Thank you so much for your interest in Stanford University, and I apologize for the mix-up with your application and the delay in getting back to you. Unfortunately, we are not able to offer you admission for our fall semester. The pool of applicants was ultracompetitive this year, and although you are extremely well qualified, we are being extra selective about our new admissions.

Your mom tells me you've been accepted to Yale and Georgetown, and I'm sure one of those schools will be extremely happy to have you.

I have sent a copy of this letter to your mailing address but wanted to make sure you had an email from me personally.

Thank you again for your interest in Stanford.

Good luck and all the best in your future endeavors.

Sincerely,

Genevieve Peletier, Admissions

I stare at the email incredulously, sure it has to be some kind of joke. Ivy League admissions humor or something? Or a prank? From Celia and Paige perhaps? I scroll back to the top of the screen and check the email address. GPeletier@stanford.edu.

I can't breathe. My face feels hot and my skin feels

prickly. There's a weird lump in my throat, and when I try to swallow it away, it feels ragged and sharp.

I take in another deep breath, but this one doesn't go that far before catching in my lungs. I think I'm having a panic attack.

"Are you okay?" Celia asks, which kind of snaps me out of it.

"Yeah," I say. "I'm fine."

But it's not true.

It's not true at all.

# T W O

OKAY. THIS IS CRAZY. FIRST OF ALL, I SHOULD
not be having this kind of extreme reaction to not getting
into Stanford. I mean, yes, it's all I've ever wanted. Yes, it's
all I've been working toward for the past four years. Yes,
my parents are going to have a complete fit and maybe disown me. But still. Having a panic attack over not getting
into a school? People have real problems, like poverty and
Alzheimer's and cancer and broken homes. Not getting into
an Ivy League school is not that big of a deal.

In fact, it's not a big deal at all. Especially when I've
already gotten into a bunch of other schools. (Well, three
other schools. But they're really good schools, so they kind
of count as a bunch.)

Plus, let's be honest. Those admissions decisions are
never the be-all and end-all. There are wait lists. And . . . all
kinds of other things you can do to get into colleges after

you've been rejected. You just need to know how to work the system. I'll bet if I call my dad, he can make a call and offer to donate some money and everything will be taken care of. Genevieve Peletier can't be the ultimate, final word in who gets to go to Stanford. If she's such a big deal, how did she find the time to email me? Someone with a lot of power doesn't email rejection letters, they make their assistant do it.

"Hello!" Paige yells, flashing her hand in front of my face. She's wearing a huge turquoise ring on her thumb, and it almost scrapes my nose. "Earth to Quinn! What's wrong?"

"Nothing." I shake my head. "I'm fine."

"You're being really weird," Celia says. She's holding her phone above her, taking a selfie against the window of the bus. She smiles and snaps the picture, then starts uploading it to her Instagram.

"Ooh," Paige says, giving me a knowing look. "Is this about Nathan?"

"Of course it's about Nathan!" Celia says. "She's freaking out because this is *the* trip."

"What?" My head feels like it's stuffed with cotton. I can't concentrate on anything these two are saying. And why is Paige being allowed to lean over the back of her seat like that? Shouldn't the bus driver tell her to sit down? It's definitely a safety hazard.

"You know, the trip where you guys either move into the

friend zone or finally hook up." Paige wiggles her eyebrows up and down.

"True," I say, mostly just to shut them up. Even Nathan Duncan can't distract me from the Stanford disaster.

Here are the important things to know about Nathan:

1.  He has dark hair and dark eyes, and he's on the swim team and plays lacrosse. He has the body to prove it—broad shoulders, a really defined chest, and the kind of muscular arms you only get from hours and hours of playing sports.
2.  He's smart and in most of my AP classes.
3.  I've known him since I was in middle school, and we've always been friendly. But then a couple of weeks ago we were at a party, and we ended up talking for most of the night while we babysat our drunk friends (me with Celia and Paige, Nathan with Ryan Moynihan and Carson Decker), and he's been super flirty with me ever since. Celia and Paige keep telling me he likes me, but I'm not sure I really believe it.

I like Nathan. He's handsome and funny and he's an awesome dresser—preppy, but not too preppy. But seriously, who can think about Nathan Carson when I just found out I didn't get into Stanford? Even if Nathan's arms *are* all ripped up with muscle, and even if he is going to Georgetown in the fall? God, maybe I should make more of an effort to find out if he really does like me. Then I can go to Georgetown, too, and when my parents throw parties, all their friends will look at me and be like, "Oh, wow, Georgetown is a great school!" and half of them will mean it, but half of them will feel sorry for me because they'll know that Gtown isn't Harvard or Yale or STANFORD.

"I heard he has a big dick," Celia says. For someone who looks so proper, she has a very dirty mouth.

"Celia!" I gasp. "Keep your voice down!"

"Oh, come on," she says. "Tell me you're not excited by that."

She giggles and then launches into a conversation about the boys in our class and who's the best in bed. Celia is much more experienced than Paige or me. She's slept with three guys so far, two of them in our class, one of them a guy she met when she went to visit her friend at college. A state school. That's what's considered slumming it in our group— having sex with a guy you met at a state school. It's actually really snobby and awful when you think about it.

I do my best to tune out their R-rated conversation until we get to the airport. As soon as I'm off the bus, I instantly start to feel better. The fresh air calms my heart and soothes my nerves.

Celia immediately grabs me and Paige by the hand and pulls us around the corner of the building, giggling the whole time. Then she reaches into her bag and pulls out the carefully rolled joint she showed us on the bus. "Come on," she says, waving it in front of my face. "You'll feel better after you take a hit. You seem really wound up. More than usual, even."

"You know I don't smoke," I say as she lights the joint and hands it to Paige. I watch as they pass it back and forth.

I wonder what will happen if we get caught. We'll probably be arrested. We definitely won't be able to go on the trip. They'll make us wait in the security office until our parents can come and bail us out. I imagine my mom, getting a call that I've been arrested for possession of marijuana. Actually, is marijuana even illegal anymore? I think it's legal if you have less than a certain amount.

But still.

We're underage.

At an airport.

I reach into my pocket and pull out my phone so I can read the email from Genevieve at Stanford again. Maybe I read it wrong. Maybe she didn't say I wasn't getting in, like for sure. Maybe she said I was going to be wait-listed. I could have hallucinated it. The brain is a very mysterious thing, especially when it comes to major life events like this.

But the email is exactly the same as I remember it.

"I'm so glad we did this," Paige is saying. She giggles.

"We can't be getting on the plane without, like, some kind of relaxation."

"Oh, totally," Celia says.

"You guys are going to get caught," I say as my phone buzzes with another email. Another email! Maybe it's from the Stanford people. Maybe there was some kind of mix-up and they realized they want me after all. Maybe they'll have to give me a scholarship or some kind of special treatment for what they've done to me. Undue mental stress and all that.

"We're not going to get caught." Paige takes the last hit off the joint, then stabs it out on the pavement with her shoe.

"Eww," Celia says. "You need to pick that up."

Paige does as she's told.

Oh. The email isn't from the Stanford people after all. It's from myself. To myself. That same email again. My hand hovers over the button, ready to delete it and send it right to the trash. But for some reason I don't. I open it and read it again.

**Before graduation, I promise to . . . *do something crazy*.**

I think about that day four years ago—Lyla, Aven, and me all sending emails to ourselves, scheduling them to repeat throughout the day so we'd make sure to take them seriously. We didn't want our future selves to think the emails were stupid because we sent them when we were only freshmen. If you'd told me that by the time the emails showed up, Lyla, Aven, and I wouldn't be friends anymore— that we wouldn't even be *speaking* to each other—I wouldn't have believed it. The thought makes me incredibly sad.

"You're being really spacey today, Quinn," Celia says. "Seriously, it's starting to worry me." She takes a bottle of Visine out of her bag and carefully squeezes a couple of drops into her eyes. She blinks and then gives me a smile. She looks so all-American it's kind of scary. Like, if this is what the youth of America is doing, we're all in trouble.

"I'm not being spacey," I say, even though I totally am.

"Girls!" a voice calls. Our class adviser, Mr. Beals, peeks around the side of the building.

"Yes, Mr. Beals?" Celia asks, like she's really interested in what he wants and wasn't just smoking pot a second ago.

"Come on, we all need to get inside," Mr. Beals says. He's already looking pretty harried, and the trip hasn't even started yet. It must be really awful to be a class adviser—you have tons of responsibility and you don't even get paid that much more. I googled it. Teachers' salaries are public record.

"Okay," I say. "We're coming."

As I pass by her, Celia pushes something into my hand. I look down. One of her Xanax, the ones she got from her doctor because she claimed to be having anxiety over her challenging course load and extracurricular activities. I shake my head at her, but she rolls her eyes.

**Before graduation, I promise to . . .** *do something crazy.*

I look down at the tiny pill in my hand.

Then I drop it onto the sidewalk, making sure to crush it into the pavement as I walk by. I'm pretty sure fourteen-year-old me wasn't talking about sharing Celia's Xanax prescription.


Once we're on the plane, Celia immediately starts in on me about Nathan.

"You need to let him know you're interested," she says.

"But why?" The thought makes my stomach turn. I don't want to have to let Nathan know I'm interested. Whatever happened to playing hard to get? Plus, I don't know how to let a guy know I'm interested. I don't know how to flirt. I'm horrible at it.

Celia gapes at me, her blue eyes turning into saucers. "Are you hearing this?" she asks Paige.

"No," Paige says. "What did she say?" She's trying to shove a bag that's way too big into the overhead compartment. A businessman who somehow got stuck on the flight with us sighs and pushes by her.

"She wants to know why she should flirt with Nathan and let him know she's interested."

"Um, because he's hot?" Paige asks, like that's the only thing that matters in this world.

"No, not because he's hot!" Celia says. She shakes her head and looks exasperated. "Seriously, you two, how are the three of us even friends?"

My thoughts exactly.

"You have to let him know you're into him because men have very fragile egos. They're not going to try to hook up with you if they think there's a chance they're going to be rejected."

I really doubt Nathan's worried about being rejected. But what do I know? I've only hooked up with one guy in my life. Richard Perkins, sophomore year. I spent so much time wondering whether I should hook up with him that by the time I did, he was pretty much over it. So maybe I should listen to Celia. Maybe she knows what she's talking about. "Okay," I say slowly. I kind of want to ask her how I'm supposed to let Nathan know I'm interested without looking like a total fool, but I don't want her to think I'm that clueless.

"Thank you," Celia says, like it's settled. "What are you going to do next year when you're at Stanford without me? I might have to Skype with you every night to make sure you don't become a social pariah."

"Ha-ha," I laugh, wondering what she would think if she knew I hadn't gotten into Stanford, if she knew I might be joining her at Yale next year after all. Probably she'd be pissed. It's rare for two people from one school to even get into Yale, and Celia likes having people think she was the only one.

I've hardly told anyone at school I got accepted to Yale, because I'm not going there. Well, *wasn't* going there. God, if I have to go to Yale, my parents are going to freak out. They have this really weird competitive thing going with their friends the Spurlocks. The Spurlocks went to Yale, and my parents *loved* telling them that even though I got into Yale, I wasn't going there. It was, like, the highlight of their lives. They'd probably rather ship me off for a year of backpacking through Europe than have to tell the Spurlocks that I'm going to Yale.

"No, seriously," Celia says. She looks me up and down. "Quinn, this is your chance. Nathan likes you."

"How do you know?" I ask. I've heard this story a billion times, but it never gets old. I mean, Nathan is really hot. And I'm only human, after all.

"Because he told me! I've told you this story, like, elev-enty million times. You don't listen to me."

"You don't," Paige agrees, finally finishing with her bag and sitting down in the row ahead of us. She leans over the back of her seat so she can hear what we're saying, just like she did on the bus. Sometimes I wonder if Paige even has her own thoughts. Like, on some level I know she must, because she's really smart. But then I see how she just parrots back everything Celia says, and I can't understand if she really means what she's saying, or if she's just saying it because she wants to stay on Celia's good side.

"I *did* listen," I say. It's true—I did listen to her story about Nathan. But what's the harm in hearing it again? Plus, I'm still a little wary. Celia tends to exaggerate, and how do I know she's not doing that now?

"We were in the library," Celia says. "And he came up to me and was like, 'What's the deal with Quinn, is she hanging out with anyone?' and I almost laughed, because it was like, 'Um, no'—no offense, Quinn—and then he was like, 'Cool,' and he got this wicked glint in his eye and was like, 'I hope I get to hang out with her on the trip.'"

"That doesn't mean he likes me," I say. I stretch my legs out into the aisle. I'm tall, and I have long legs, and they always get cramped up during plane rides. Beckett Cross goes walking by, bumping his bag right into me. God. What a jerk. "Watch it," I say irritably.

"Sorry," he says, and grins.

As he passes, I catch a glimpse of the tag on the bag he's holding. *Lyla McAfee*, it says in pink script. What the hell is Beckett Cross doing with Lyla's bag? Lyla's been dating this guy Derrick for, like, ever. Did they break up? I turn to watch Beckett as he carries the bag to the back of the plane, but before I can see where he's going, the pilot comes over the speaker and tells everyone to get ready for takeoff.

I lean back and buckle my seat belt. I hate the taking-off

part of the flight. Most crashes take place during the take-off or the landing, so I can never really relax until we're in the air. Of course, even then I can't *completely* relax, because there's still the landing part to deal with.

"It *does* mean that he likes you," Celia says. "It means that he loves you and he wants to have, like, five million babies with you." She giggles. "Or at least make out with you on the beach."

"I'm not sure if I want to make out with him," I say, even though I'm pretty sure I do. I clutch the armrests as hard as I can as the plane starts off down the runway.

"Yes, you do," Celia says.

"You definitely do," Paige calls over the back of her seat.

Celia looks at the way I'm clutching the seat. "Actually, I don't think you have any idea what you want. You should have taken the Xanax I offered you. You're a mess."

"Thanks," I say sarcastically.

"You're welcome."

Celia takes out her headphones. Once the plane is safely in the air, I push my seat back a little and close my eyes. I must have fallen asleep, because the next thing I know, the plane is coming in for a bumpy landing. I sit up and look around wildly, my heart pounding.

"Hey, hey, hey," someone says. "You're fine. Just relax."

The voice is coming from next to me, but it's not Celia's or Paige's voice.

It's a male voice. A deep male voice.

Nathan Duncan is sitting next to me.

I look down.

He's holding my hand.

Nathan Duncan. Is. Holding. My. Hand.

# THREE

THE THING ABOUT WAKING UP ON A PLANE
with one of the most popular guys in school holding your
hand is that if you're me, it doesn't happen. And I'm not saying that in an "Oh my god, I don't know how cute I am"
Jennifer Lawrence kind of way. It seriously just does not happen. It's the kind of thing that would happen to Celia, or
Paige, or probably a million other girls. But not me.

I'm completely out of my element. So of course I do
something completely stupid. I pull my hand away. Which is
really rude. And not the kind of thing you do when you wake
up holding the hand of a superhot guy. And besides, he has
a really nice hand. Very comforting.

"Oh, sorry," Nathan says, "I probably shouldn't have
done that. You just seemed a little disoriented. I guess it was
instinct. I didn't mean to scare you."

He grins at me, and my heart melts. He doesn't seem like

he's insecure or has a fragile ego, or whatever it is Celia said about men. In fact, if he's hurt that I've taken my hand away, he doesn't show it. He's probably not used to being rejected, so it, like, doesn't even register to him. Not that I was rejecting him. Was I rejecting him? I'm not . . . I don't . . . I feel hot and confused. This whole trip is just starting off way too weird.

I wonder if I'm in a dream. A dream where I haven't gotten into Stanford and where I wake up holding Nathan Duncan's hand. Although that would be very weird—to have a dream where you wake up.

"Um, that's okay," I say.

"I asked Celia if we could trade seats. Sorry I freaked you out." He has really long legs—even longer than mine—and his knees are pushed up against the back of the seat. "Are you okay?" His light-blue eyes are looking at me with concern. "You were mumbling and getting really tense."

"Oh yeah, I'm fine," I say. Mumbling and getting tense? What was I mumbling? And what does that mean, exactly, getting tense? Like, my body was getting tense? An image of my back getting stiff and my torso convulsing like the exorcist runs through my mind. How humiliating. I reach up and smooth my hair, then run the back of my hand over my chin. Sometimes I drool when I sleep, and the last thing I want is for Nathan to see that.

The plane bounces and skitters down the runway before slowing to a stop. I just sit there, not really sure what to do now. Should I get up and let him by? Or is this where I'm supposed to let him know that I'm interested?

"Where's Celia now?" I ask.

"A few rows up." He leans down so that his head is touching the back of the seat ahead of us. "I didn't know you were sleeping. Otherwise I wouldn't have asked to switch with her."

"Oh." I swallow and try to think of something else to say to him. Now that I'm coming out of my fog, I realize that the flight is over. Yay for not crashing! Of course, the odds of dying in a plane crash are something like one in eleven million, and your odds of dying in a car crash are one in four thousand. And yet I get in a car all the time. The brain really does work in mysterious ways.

I try to focus it on coming up with something flirty to say to Nathan. Am I ruining my chance? My chance is passing me by! People on the plane are starting to get up and grab their stuff. Someone almost hits me in the head with their suitcase. I can't think of anything to say! I'm just sitting here like an idiot!

Finally I take a big deep breath and then stand up, because honestly, what else am I supposed to do? I can't just sit here forever.

"Is this your bag?" Nathan asks, standing up next to me and grabbing the one in the overhead compartment.

"Yes," I say, and he hands it to me. Standing here next to him, I realize how tall he is. He towers over me. He smiles at me again. Say something, Quinn! But I'm blank. I've got nothing.

From the front of the plane, one of Nathan's friends calls his name. "I should go," he says. "But maybe I'll see you later?"

"Yeah," I say. "Of course." I try to emphasize the last part, so he knows I'm definitely interested. But he doesn't seem to really catch on.

He takes a step toward the front of the plane, and then he's gone.

My phone buzzes.

That stupid email again.

Before graduation, I promise to . . . *do something crazy*.

It's a sign! I should have asked him to hang out. I should have done something.

But then I shake my head. That's the last thing I need to do.

My future is completely in jeopardy. I haven't gotten into Stanford. And doing something crazy isn't going to help me. At all.

\* \* \*

By the time I walk into the lobby of our hotel, I'm actually starting to feel a lot better. About everything. Yes, that performance with Nathan wasn't stellar, but it's not like I did anything horrible. And he did say he wanted to hang out with me later. So I'll have a chance to redeem myself.

And as for the Stanford thing, yes, it's a problem, but really all I need is a plan. I'm sure there's someone else I can talk to, or an appeals process I can go through. I'll probably just have to go in for an extra interview or something. Maybe I can even make charts and graphs, the kind that will prove I'm way more qualified than some of the other people they let in. I'll do a PowerPoint and knock their socks off with how science-minded I am.

"Ugh," Celia says, sitting down next to me in one of the hotel conference rooms. Our whole class is meeting here so Mr. Beals can go over the rules with us. "This trip is already ridiculous."

"Where have you been?" I demand.

After I got off the plane, I caught a glimpse of Celia at the airport, but then we got separated in the crowd.

"Just around," she says breezily. "I tried to find you on the airport shuttle bus, but I think we got on two different ones." She lets out a big sigh, like she can't believe how hard her life is. "Did you hear that Paige and I got stuck rooming with Katie Wells? Like, how annoying is that? She's the worst. All she wants to talk about is herself and her horses. Her *horses,* Quinn. The girl is seventeen years old and she still rides horses. I mean, we're not in middle school anymore. Get a new hobby."

She reaches up and fiddles with her fake eyelashes, making sure they're still connected to her real ones. Celia gets eyelash extensions put on, but she didn't have time to get them refilled before we left for Florida, so she's wearing falsies. I hope they're waterproof.

"What?" I ask, confused. "I thought I was rooming with you and Paige." A couple of weeks ago we had to fill out a form and indicate roommate preferences for the trip. Of course Celia and Paige and I all put that we wanted to room together. Since there were supposed to be three people to a room, we figured it was a given we'd get matched up.

"Yeah, well, somebody must have screwed up." Celia takes in a deep breath. "I tried to talk to Mr. Beals about it, but he's being totally and completely unreasonable. He didn't even want to listen to what I had to say. Apparently someone on this trip has ringworm and he's, like, completely consumed with it."

"What?"

"Yeah. Some kid named Bruno. He allegedly got it from wrestling, but can you imagine? It's, like, highly contagious." She looks down at her arms, as if checking them for any kind of disease, but of course her skin is perfect as always. "Anyway, you should check your room assignment and see who you're with."

On the bus on the way here they handed out papers to everyone that listed their room numbers and roommates. I hadn't even looked at mine, because I just assumed I'd be with Celia and Paige. I rummage through my bag and pull out the paper. *Quinn Reynolds,* it says, *room 217.* When I see the names underneath my own, my heart sinks.

*Aven Shepard.*

*Lyla McAfee.*

What? How did I end up rooming with Lyla and Aven? Those two are the very last people in the whole wide world I'd want to room with. In fact, if I had to fill out a form that asked me who my very last choices were, I would have written Lyla McAfee and Aven Shepard. Seriously, I'd rather room with Ringworm Bruno than Lyla or Aven.

"Who was in charge of making these room assignments?" I demand.

"I dunno." Celia shrugs. "But don't even think about asking someone to change them. They won't do it." She shakes her head and drums her fingers on the table, impatient for the meeting to begin.

I look back down at the paper in front of me.

Lyla. Aven. Me. All in the same room. The last time

the three of us were in close proximity, we ended up in a fight. A wave of guilt sears through my body, the kind of guilt that burns like an inferno, the kind of guilt you don't want to have to face for even one second, because if you do, you might have to confront the fact that you're a horrible person.

I take in a deep breath and do what I always do whenever I think about Lyla and Aven—I push them out of my mind. But then I spot something at the bottom of the paper I'm holding.

From the Office of the Student Action Committee.

The Student Action Committee is a committee I actually thought about joining, because I thought it would look good on my Stanford application. (Ha-ha.) But then I realized I'd be better off doing debate and tennis, because it would make me seem more well-rounded. (Intellectual and athletic!)

And even though the Student Action Committee *sounds* very impressive, they actually don't really do that much. They meet once a week in the library and try to implement programs for the student body. But I think all they really do is sit around and *talk* about stuff they want to implement, because they don't seem to really get anything done. They spend most of their time doing clerical work and other busywork for all the different school events—like adding up money for fund-raisers, or making room assignments for our senior trip.

So I didn't join. For all those reasons. But if I'm being completely honest, one of the other (main?) reasons I didn't join was because Aven is on the committee.

As Mr. Beals takes his place at the front of the conference room and starts talking about the rules for the trip (which are completely ridiculous and self-explanatory—like not spending the night in other people's rooms, not partaking in alcohol and drugs—pretty much everything everyone's going to do anyway), I let my eyes wander around the room until I spot Aven.

She's sitting in the corner at one of the round tables, her dark hair pulled back from her face. She's pretending to listen to Mr. Beals, but she seems a little distracted—her leg is bouncing up and down under the table, and she keeps chewing on one of her fingernails. She looks nervous. Is it because she knows she's going to be rooming with me and Lyla? Or is it because she set us up to be roommates on purpose?

She must have. There's no way she was on that committee and the three of us just *happened* to end up rooming together. It's way too random.

But why would Aven want us all to room together? She's not expecting the three of us to become friends again, is she? If so, she's more delusional than I thought. I keep watching as she twists her hands in her lap and then glances toward the table next to her. I flick my eyes over to see what she's looking at. Liam Marsh. The guy she's been obsessed with for, like, ever. Supposedly they're best friends, but Aven's always been secretly in love with him.

Before graduation, I will . . . *tell the truth*.

That's what Aven wrote in her email to herself. It was ambiguous, but Lyla and I both knew exactly what Aven was talking about—finally telling Liam she wanted to be more than friends.

Of course, I thought it was a terrible idea. You don't just go around telling your guy friends you're in love with them. There's no point. If a guy likes you, he doesn't just continue being friends with you. He makes a move. It's definitely a misconception that guys won't go after you because they don't want to ruin the friendship. Puh-leeze. Guys don't care about friendships. They care about sex. And if they think they can get it from someone they're even remotely interested in, they go for it. Whether they're friends or not.

But when Aven wrote that email, I didn't try to talk her

out of it—I was sure that by the time we were seniors, the whole Liam situation would have been resolved, one way or the other. I figured the most likely scenario was that they wouldn't even be friends anymore, or if they were that Aven would have gotten over her ridiculous crush. But from the way she's looking at Liam, it's apparent she hasn't.

As Mr. Beals drones on and on about the signs of ring-worm, I scan the crowd of my classmates for Lyla until I spot her on the other side of the room, looking agitated and impatient.

Could she have had something to do with the room assignments? I don't think so. If Aven and Lyla had worked together to make sure we all roomed together, that would mean they were friends again. The thought of the two of them becoming friends without me makes my stomach squeeze. But if they *were* friends again, wouldn't they have just roomed with each other? Unless they wanted to make up with me, too. But then why didn't they just approach me? They could have asked me to talk, sent me a text or an email or something.

Plus, if they were friends again, they'd probably be sit-ting together. No. This is definitely Aven working alone. I can't believe how nervy she is. Especially for someone who lives her life being so afraid of everything.

My phone vibrates.

Before graduation, I promise to . . . *do something crazy*.

Well. Rooming with Lyla and Aven certainly fits the bill.


Once the meeting is over, the conference room erupts into complete and total pandemonium. Kids are talking and laughing, bags are being rolled over the floor, and everyone's pushing toward the exit. Our whole class is jazzed up from sitting so long, and they're anxious to get out into the sunshine and start the trip.

"Meet in our room in fifteen," Celia instructs. "We're gonna hit the beach, okay? Nathan will probably be there, so wear your black bikini." She grabs my hand and then twirls under it, like we're ballroom dance partners or something.

I giggle in spite of myself. This *is* vacation, after all. And the beach sounds awesome right now.

"See you in a little," Celia says. She and Paige disappear down the hallway toward their room. I sigh and wish I were going with them. I think about heading back into the conference room and begging Mr. Beals to let me change my room assignment. But I know it's probably not going to happen.

Whatever. Just because Lyla and Aven and I are going to be in the same room doesn't mean that I have to hang out with them. In fact, I probably won't even see them. It's my senior trip. I'm not going to be sitting in my room the whole time—I'm going to be out and about, having fun.

My phone starts ringing in my bag, and I reach in and rummage around for it. It's my brother, Neal.

"Hey," I say, as I start wandering down the hall toward the elevator bank. There's a crowd of kids from my class doing the same thing, so I linger a little longer near the lobby, deciding to wait until things thin out a bit. "What's up?"

Neal's a sophomore at Stanford, but he's home for spring break. Neal and I are pretty close—well, as close as you can be to your older brother. I always secretly wished Neal had been a girl, so I could raid his closet and talk to him about boys. Of course, everyone I know who has a sister wishes they had a brother, because their sisters are always stealing their clothes and being bitchy to them. Also, they think that if you have an older brother, he brings home his hot friends and then you get to hook up with them.

Neal does have a lot of hot friends, but I've never hooked up with any of them. One, because I don't have time for that. And two, because, well, none of them has ever really shown any interest in me. (Actually, that's not true—last year Neal brought his freshman roommate, Brody, home over Thanksgiving. After dinner Brody cornered me in the hallway and asked if I wanted to party in his room late night. Then he raised his eyebrows up and down, like he wanted to make it clear exactly what kind of partying he was talking about. Which it was, because he was making it so skeezily obvious. Actually, now that I think about it, I probably should have told my parents and made them kick him out, because that was extremely inappropriate. Oh well. He and Neal aren't friends anymore—Brody dropped out of Stanford over the summer and never came back. I think he was on drugs.)

"Not much," Neal says. "I just wanted to let you know you have a letter here from Stanford."

My stomach does a back handspring, and a lump forms in my throat. A letter? From Stanford? Genevieve said she wasn't going to send it out for a few days! Didn't she? Or did she just say a copy of her email was soon to follow? Why is my normally perfect memory failing me now? Maybe it's blocking out traumatic experiences, like how accident victims can't remember anything about getting hurt.

Suddenly, something about a letter arriving at my house seems almost . . . ominous. An email is one thing—people are always firing off emails at a moment's notice without worrying about what's in them.

But a letter sounds official. An official admissions letter. On real, actual paper. Probably with the school seal and a masthead. It sounds like the kind of thing that would have to be logged somewhere. Up until this point, I was kind of hoping maybe I could just email Genevieve and try to get her to change her mind, or at least find out who else I could talk to. Now that a letter's been sent, it's a whole different ball game.

Although . . . maybe the letter isn't from the admissions office at all. Maybe it's just one of those pamphlets they send urging you to apply to their school. That would be ironic—them inviting me to apply when they've just rejected me.

"Oh," I say to Neal, trying my best to keep my voice light. "Who's it from?"

"Stanford. I just said that."

"No, I mean . . . what department at Stanford?"

"Admissions," he says. He sounds exasperated, like he can't believe I'm asking so many questions. "It's probably your acceptance letter."

Or not.

"Oh," I say. "That's great."

"Why are you being weird?"

A bunch of kids from my school go walking by, talking excitedly. They're being pretty loud and obnoxious, but for once I'm actually glad they're acting that way. I need some time to stall so I can figure out what the hell I'm going to say to my brother.

"Hold on," I say, then take my time moving to a corner of the lobby that's a little quieter. I take in a deep breath, like they taught us to do in this yoga class we had to take in gym. "I'm back!" I say finally, trying to inject some enthusiasm into my voice. "Thanks for calling me! Sorry if I was being weird, we just got to the hotel and there were a lot of people around."

"Oh, okay." Neal accepts this explanation, because he is a boy and boys have simple emotions. Score one more point for having a brother. "So do you want me to open it or not?"

"No!" I practically scream. "I mean, um, I don't think so. No, thanks."

"*No?*"

"No. Ah, I think I should wait until I get home so I can do it myself."

"Are you sure? That's going to be, like, three more days. Don't you want to know what it says?" Not really.

"Of course I want to know what it says. But I want to open it myself. You know, to have the moment." My words sound hollow in my ears, and I'm afraid I'm losing control of the situation. I try to think about what I would do if I hadn't gotten that email this morning, if I didn't already know that I didn't get into Stanford. Probably I would have let Neal open the letter. But that's not an option. And then I have a brilliant idea. "Send it to me!" I crow.

"What?" Neal sounds startled, probably because I sound manic.

"Send it to me! The letter! Overnight it to me, here at the hotel."

"Really?" He sounds doubtful. "Don't you want to open it in front of Mom and Dad?"

Ha. Ha. Ha-ha! "Well, obviously, you know, that would be *ideal*." In a nightmare. "But since I'm not home, I don't want to have to wait days. So if you could just overnight it to me, then I could open it. Maybe I'll have someone take a video of me doing it, and then I'll send it to Mom and Dad. You know, like a surprise."

"I don't know, Quinn," he says. "You know Mom and Dad don't like surprises. They'll probably be upset they didn't get to see you open your letter."

"What are you talking about? Mom and Dad love surprises." My phone buzzes with a text, and I look down at it. Celia. *u almost ready for the beach?* I quickly type back, *almost! txt u when I'm ready!* I add a smiley emoticon at the end, and one of those emojis of a palm tree. I hate emoticons, and the only reason I even have them on my phone is because Paige downloaded them one day without my knowledge. She and Celia think it's hilarious how much I hate them, and they did it to annoy me. For a while they were sending me messages strictly in emojis, leaving me to try and decipher them.

"They do not love surprises," Neal is saying. "Remember

when Mom threw Dad a surprise birthday party? He really didn't like it."

"Yes, he did."

"No, he just *pretended* to like it, but inside he really didn't. He thought it was over the top, and it made him feel awkward."

"Did he tell you that?"

"Not in so many words."

"Neal, first of all, Dad did like that surprise party. And second of all, a surprise party is different from a video surprise from his daughter."

"How?"

"*How?*"

"Yes, how is it different? They're both fundamentally the same thing. They're both going to pop up on him out of nowhere."

"My video will not pop up on him out of nowhere! My acceptance letter is totally expected. It's all I've been talking about for, like, my whole life."

"Yes, but . . ." As Neal starts prattling on about the reasons he thinks it's a bad idea, I marvel at the fact that I'm having an argument with my brother over something so stupid. Actually, that's not really the weird part. My family gets into debates over things all the time—affirmative action, gay marriage, what an object really is, whether boys should be encouraged to like pink. We're a very debatey family. It's how we connect. But to be having an annoying debate like this with my brother, over something that's not even going to happen, is a whole new level of ridiculousness.

"Neal!" I say finally. "I hear what you're saying, and thank you for your thoughts on whether Mom and Dad like surprises. I will take them all into consideration before I decide what to do. But in the meantime, could you please overnight the letter to me?" I say a quick prayer of thanks that the days of thick envelopes and skinny envelopes are over. Nowadays colleges don't send you a big packet if you've been accepted. They just send you a letter with a link to a pdf file that has all the info.

"Fine," Neal says, sounding miffed. "What's the address?"

I spot a hotel notepad sitting on one of the tables in the lobby, and I rattle off the address that's printed on the bottom, then give him my room number. "Thanks," I say before hanging up.

My phone buzzes again, and I look down, about to tell Celia and Paige that I'm hurrying and to stop bothering me.

But it's not a text.

It's my email.

From myself to myself.

**Before graduation, I promise to . . .** *do something crazy.*

I shake my head and delete it. Again.

Begging my brother to send me my rejection letter, all the while making him believe it's an acceptance letter, is crazy enough for me.

# FOUR

WHEN I FINALLY GET UP TO MY ROOM, LYLA IS sitting on one of the beds, looking around in confusion. There are two queen-size beds on either side of the room, and a twin-size cot set up in the corner. Lyla's bags are sitting on the floor near the bed she's sitting on, almost like she's claiming it. Not that I blame her—who the hell wants to sleep on a cot? I thought for sure I'd end up having to be the one to do it, since I took so much time downstairs. But it looks like Aven hasn't gotten here yet.

Lyla looks up, her eyes meeting mine. My chest tightens, and a flash of sadness flows through me. For the briefest moment, and for some unexplainable reason, I wish more than anything that I was going to the beach with Lyla and Aven, and not Celia and Paige.

But that's ridiculous. One, because it could never happen. Lyla and Aven and I aren't friends anymore. Lyla wants nothing to do with me, and if I'm being honest, I don't blame her. What I did to her was . . . well, it was awful. But thinking about that doesn't serve any kind of purpose, and besides, it's not like she was innocent in the whole situation.

So I just look at her and say, "You've got to be kidding me." Then I drop my suitcase on the floor and walk into the bathroom. I take deep breaths and splash some cold water on my face. I am strong, I am confident, I am in control. I repeat the mantra to myself and then return to the room.

I intentionally avoid Lyla's gaze. Her eyes are this deep, rich brown, the kind of eyes that change color depending on her mood or the lighting, going from dark to light back to dark again. I remember when we had our fight how I couldn't stop looking at her eyes, how I could tell she was really mad by the way they kept changing, like flashing lights warning me to back off. But I couldn't stop it. The damage was already done. And even though I kept trying to reach out to her, it didn't matter. She was done with me. And Aven, too.

Whatever. I have enough to worry about right now without thinking about that. It's in the past. I pick up my suitcase and drop it onto the other bed. *I will not look at Lyla, I will not look at Lyla, I will not look at Lyla.* It's taking every single ounce of my willpower not to ask her what she's been up to, if she ever thinks about me and Aven, if she got the email she sent herself and if she's going to do what it says.

"I'm assuming you took that bed?" I ask instead. I'm

trying so hard not to let her see how flustered I am that my tone sounds a little harsher than I intended.

"Um, well, I'm not sure," Lyla says. "I mean, I didn't want to take it before everyone else got here, so I just thought that maybe—"

"Well, whatever," I say. "You can have it. Let Aven sleep on the cot."

"Aven?"

"Yeah." I'm rummaging through my bag, looking for my bathing suit. I finally find it buried under a pile of tank tops. I pull it out, along with my cover-up and flip-flops. "She's our third roommate."

"You have got to be kidding me." She sounds genuinely shocked. How did she not know that Aven was our roommate? Did she not look at the paper they gave us on the bus?

"Yup." I shake my head. "Apparently she's still living in fantasy world."

Lyla frowns and pushes her hair back from her face. "What do you mean?"

"Aven was in charge of making the room assignments. She's on the Student Action Committee." I feel bad for a second, because I don't know for sure Aven's the one who made the room assignments. But what are the chances she didn't? There's no way we just randomly got selected to be put together. No way.

"The Student Action Committee?" Lyla's asking. "I've

never even heard of the Student Action Committee."

"That's not surprising," I say. What I mean is that she's probably never heard of it because the Student Action Committee is worthless, but Lyla looks like she's been slapped. And then I realize she must think I mean she doesn't pay attention to anything, and that's why she's never heard of it. I open my mouth to explain. But then I think, so what if she thinks I said something bitchy to her? I tried to reach out to Lyla so many times, I sent her text after text after text for days after our fight, only to be ignored. Why should I feel bad for being a little bratty to someone who treated me like that?

"What's that supposed to mean?" Lyla asks. She sounds halfway defensive, and halfway like she really wants to know.

"Nothing, just that sometimes you don't pay attention to what's going on." Like when I'm passing her in the halls at school and she's totally consumed with her boyfriend, Derrick. Seriously, it's so annoying. I'm sure they're like ohmygod totally in love, but really? Do they have to walk around holding hands like lovesick puppies? Actually, lovesick puppies don't hold hands—they just stare at each other with love. But I've never seen Derrick and Lyla staring at each other with love. At least not in a while. Are those two having problems? I remember how Beckett Cross was carrying her bag on the plane, and I wonder if there's something going on between the two of them.

"Yeah," Lyla says. "And sometimes *you* pay *too* much

attention to what's going on."

I open my mouth to let her know her remark makes no sense, that there's no way someone can pay *too* much attention to what's going on. I mean, seriously? But then I realize what she means. That I told her secret. That I screwed everything up. That if I'm being completely honest with myself, the real reason Aven, Lyla, and I aren't friends anymore is because of me.

It's not one of those "oh, everyone had a part in it, it's a complicated situation" kind of things. It's *my* fault. *I* told Lyla's secret. *I* betrayed her. And I can't take that back. But instead of dealing with any of that, I close my mouth and march into the bathroom, where I change into my bathing suit and cover-up.

When I come back into the room, I make a big show of unpacking my stuff and placing it in my drawers. I'm already late to meet Celia and Paige for the beach, but I don't care. I want to give Lyla a chance to say something else to me.

But she just makes some snide remark about how I'm unpacking my clothes at a hotel, which is a ridiculous thing to make a snide remark about, because honestly, who *doesn't* unpack their clothes at a hotel? What is she going to do with hers, just leave them in her suitcase? That's a horrible idea. They'll get all wrinkled. And how will she be able to find anything? She'll have to go pawing through her suitcase every time she wants to change.

I'm just finishing up when a key card slides into the door and Aven comes strolling in. She looks around the room and sees me putting my stuff into the dresser by one bed and Lyla sitting on the other. I wait for her to freak out about the fact that we stuck her with the cot.

"I guess I'm taking the cot," she says happily. Wow. She doesn't even have the decency to look guilty about how she manipulated things and got us all put in the same room. Talk about an abuse of power. I'll bet if I told Mr. Beals about this, he'd totally kick her off the committee. I think about marching downstairs and telling him right now, just to be a brat. Then maybe he'd fix it and I could go back to being roommates with Paige and Celia and not have this whole vacation be a total nightmare.

"I think we could all benefit from spending some time together," Aven says when she realizes that Lyla and I are just staring at her incredulously. "I know that our misunderstanding got out of hand, but with graduation coming up, I think it might really be time to move past it."

For a second, a weird kind of hope blooms in my chest. Are we going to talk about this? Like, really talk about what happened? Here? Now? Are we going to maybe work it out?

But Lyla just laughs bitterly. "Is that what you think it was? A misunderstanding?"

"I know your feelings are still probably really hurt, Lyla,"

Aven says, her tone serious. "But Quinn and I never meant to hurt you."

"Don't speak for me," I say automatically. I *didn't* mean to hurt Lyla—in fact, it was the last thing I wanted to do. How was I supposed to know that telling her secret was going to end up in disaster? When I did it, I didn't realize what the consequences were going to be. But letting Aven talk for me is a bad idea, since the reason we're in this mess in the first place is because of everyone talking behind each other's backs.

Lyla glares at me. "So you *did* mean to hurt me?"

I resist the urge to roll my eyes. Why is she so angry all the time? So defensive? What does she think, that people never get into fights? She never even gave me a *chance* to explain, even though I tried to talk to her dozens and dozens of times. So maybe this whole thing *wasn't* completely my fault. If Lyla had just given me an opportunity to explain, maybe we could have worked it out. Suddenly getting into this right now seems extremely exhausting and a complete waste of time. To do the same things over and over again, hoping for a different outcome, really is the definition of insanity.

"Whatever," I say. "I don't want to do this. I don't even *care* about this. It takes up, like, this amount of space in my mind." I hold my fingers an inch apart, so they can see how little I think of it. It's a half lie. I try not to think about the two of them that much, but only because it's way too painful.

And then, before they can say anything else, I turn and walk out the door. I'm suddenly super angry at both of them. How dare Lyla not give me a chance to explain when we first had that fight? And how dare Aven set us all up to be in the same room? This is our senior trip, too, and she knows Lyla and I wouldn't have wanted the three of us to be roommates. Talk about being selfish.

I open the door to the room and poke my head back in. "Keep your hands off my stuff, Aven," I say. "I know you like to borrow people's things." Then I give them both this really big fake smile and slam the door.

I stand out in the hallway for a moment, not moving. I thought snapping at them like that would make me feel better, would make me feel like I had at least a little bit of control of the situation. But it didn't. In fact, it just made me feel worse.

*Go back in. Apologize. Maybe we really can work this out.*

My phone buzzes.

Paige.

**Where r u?!?!**

I sigh and head for the elevator bank. Quinn and Aven are a part of my past. And that's where they're going to stay.

***

When I get to Paige and Celia's room, Celia is already tipsy, and Paige is looking at her in thinly veiled disgust.

"How are we going to get her downstairs and past Mr. Beals?" Paige asks as soon as I walk in.

We both glance over at Celia. She's sitting on her bed, talking to someone on the phone and painting her toenails bright red. When she sees me, she breaks into a huge smile and then hangs up on the person she's talking to without even saying good-bye.

"Quinny!" she says, even though she knows I hate that nickname. "What took you so long?"

"I was getting ready," I say, deciding not to get into the fact that I was trying to avoid a fight with my ex–best friends and freaking out about my official Stanford rejection letter, which has apparently just arrived at my home and fallen into the possession of my unreliable older brother. "What have you been doing?"

She looks around. "Shhh!" she says. Then she reaches under the bed and pulls out a bottle of Corona. "I got this. From a guy." She giggles.

"From a guy?" I look at Paige, who shrugs.

"Some guy was coming door-to-door asking if we wanted to buy beer," she says. "I think he was one of the local college kids, trying to make a buck."

"And you let her buy some?" I take the Corona out of Celia's hand and study it for signs of tampering. "Are you crazy? That's how girls end up raped and dead in the woods." What is *wrong* with the two of them? I mean, seriously.

"Oh, relax," Celia says. She waves the nail-polish brush in the air, and little drops of red polish fly off and drop onto the white comforter. "I made sure the bottles were still sealed." She caps the polish and starts blowing on her toes. "I'm not stupid."

And that's the thing. She really *isn't* stupid. She just makes really bad decisions. "How much have you had to drink?" I ask.

"Only one and a half, Mom," she says. When she sees the look Paige is giving her, she throws her hands up in the air. "Oh my god, not you too, Paige!" Hmm. What's that supposed to mean? That she expects me to be lame, but she can't take the idea that Paige might give her a hard time, too? "I thought you *wanted* to buy the beer!"

"I did, but I didn't want to start drinking it right away. I thought we'd at least save it for later."

"We have plenty for later," Celia says. She motions us over and lifts up the comforter on one side of the bed. Three six-packs stare back at us. "Can you believe he was charging fifty dollars a six-pack?" She throws herself back on the bed and giggles. "Not that I care. I think he was surprised I didn't try to haggle."

For the first time, I say a quick prayer of thanks that I'm not rooming with Celia and Paige. If I got caught with alcohol in my room, there's no way I'd be allowed into Stanford. I'd get sent home from the trip and it would appear on my permanent record. I know because it was all over the informational packet they sent us—that if anyone got caught with alcohol, it would go on our permanent records and any colleges we'd applied to would be notified. Say what you want about Lyla and Aven—but at least I won't have to worry about them bringing beer into our room and getting me kicked out of school.

But Celia and Paige don't really think about things like that. They can hardly even fathom the idea they might get caught, and they figure that even if by some small chance they do, nothing will really happen. They think rules are just scare tactics.

I sigh. "Are we going to the beach or not?" They were bothering me to rush down here, and they're not even ready.

"Of course." Celia hops off the bed. "Just let me pee real quick."

She passes by us in a cloud of perfume.

Paige looks at me.

I shrug. "She's tipsy, yeah, but I don't think it's that

noticeable, as long as we don't stop to talk to anyone."

"Okay."

Celia emerges from the bathroom looking fresh as a daisy. Her hair is smooth, and she's wearing a pink-and-orange paisley bikini, with no cover-up.

"Aren't you going to wear something over that?" Paige asks.

"Why?" Celia twirls around and checks out her butt in the mirror. "Does it make me look fat?"

"No, but do you really want to be parading around in just a bikini?"

"Yes," Celia says very adamantly. Then she giggles and hiccups. "I want to get tan all over. In fact, I wish I didn't even have to *wear* a bathing suit."

Paige and I exchange a look. Celia wouldn't actually try to get naked on the beach, would she? If she did, there would really be no way to stop her. But we'd have to try. There's a difference between Celia doing her normal crazy stuff, and her getting nude in front of our whole class after she's had a few drinks. Although if I'm being completely honest, she doesn't seem like the alcohol is really affecting her that much. Drunk Celia isn't really that much different from Sober Celia.

"Come on, Mustang Sally," I say, shaking my head. "Let's go."

When we get down to the beach, my mood instantly

lightens. The sun is shining bright in the sky, the air is salty and humid, and the sand is cool against my feet. The water is blue and sparkling, the waves calm and soothing. It's gorgeous, and exactly what I need to relax my mind and focus my intentions.

I decide that after I put my towel down, I'll get to work composing an email to Genevieve in admissions. I thought about calling her, but then I decided an email is definitely better. I can make it sound very professional. And I can ask her when a good time would be to call her and discuss the appeals process for her decision. Maybe I should even put in a little dig about how since my application got lost, that maybe I really shouldn't be penalized, and that maybe a lot of well-qualified students had their applications go missing and how maybe the media might be interested in that story.

I'll bet some reporter somewhere would want to cover it. How my application got lost and so other less qualified applicants got in, thereby putting Stanford's pristine reputation in jeopardy? It's totally one of those stories that could go viral on BuzzFeed. I even have a bunch of pictures my mom took of me in a Stanford onesie when I was a baby. I could include those to give the story a good human interest angle.

I lie back on my towel and adjust the straw hat I'm wearing before slathering more sunscreen onto my legs. I have very fair skin, and I burn super easily. Sometimes if I'm even just walking around outside for a few minutes, I get red.

Celia lies down next to me and immediately falls asleep. I can't tell if she's passed out from the beers, or just tired. I look at Paige, kind of like, *Should we wake her up?* But she just shrugs, and so I decide to let it go. How much trouble can Celia really get into if she's sleeping? And I *told* her to put sunscreen on, but she didn't listen. She said she wanted to get color. So if she gets burned, it's her own fault.

Paige pulls a bunch of magazines out of her bag and spreads them out on her blanket. I take one and pretend to be paging through it, but the whole time my mind is working on composing an email to Genevieve.

Finally I pull my phone out and surreptitiously type away, letting Genevieve know that I appreciate her decision and that I understand that my application was late, but that it was through no fault of my own, and that I don't think it's fair that people who are underqualified got in over me. (I decide to leave out the part about the media being interested in the story, because honestly I don't want to threaten her right away. If she gives me crap after this, then maybe I'll go there.)

I proofread the email, then hit send.

I take in a deep breath. There's a definite satisfaction that comes after you've done a task. I wish I'd made a to-do list and put "email Genevieve" on it. Then I could cross it right off.

My phone rings then. Could Genevieve be calling already? I'm very good with the written word, but I didn't realize I was that good! Oh. It's not Genevieve. It's Neal. Probably calling with an updated argument on why I shouldn't send my parents a video of me opening up my nonexistent acceptance letter.

"Hello?"

"Hey," he says. "What are you doing?"

"Lying on the beach, listening to the waves, relaxing . . . What are you doing?"

"Nothing, really." Pause.

"Okay." He still doesn't say anything. "Well, are you calling for a reason?"

"Of course I'm calling for a reason, Quinn. We just talked an hour ago. Why would I be calling you back already if I didn't have a reason?"

"Okay, so then what is it?" Seriously, you'd think for someone who has higher-than-average verbal skills, he'd be a little better at communicating.

"So something bad happened." Wow. I guess higher-than-average verbal skills don't leave time for beating around the bush.

"Like what?"

"Like I went to get your acceptance letter, and it's gone."

"What do you mean it's *gone*?" From next to me, Paige looks up from her magazine and gives me a quizzical look.

I roll my eyes and mouth "my crazy brother," then get up and move away from her so she won't be able to overhear my conversation. I really do not want Paige finding out I got a letter from Stanford. Or Celia for that matter, even if she is passed out on her towel.

"Tell Neal I said hi!" Paige calls after me. "Tell him I miss him!" Paige has a huge crush on my brother, for reasons that are not completely clear to any sane person. Supposedly a lot of girls think my brother is a hottie. Which is another pitfall of having an older brother—your friends think they should be able to date him, which is ridiculous. I don't want my friends dating my brother. That's disturbing.

"Is that Paige?" my brother asks. "Tell her I said hi back." My brother's not even remotely interested in Paige—he just likes the fact that she's interested in him, so he flirts with her constantly. Typical jerky guy.

I walk a few more yards down the beach.

"He says hi back," I say to the ocean.

"What did she say?" he asks.

"She said she wants to have five babies with you," I say. "She said she's going to stop taking her birth control pills right now, that she's going to—"

"Paige is on the pill?" Neal asks.

"Neal!" I say. "Can you please focus here? What do you mean, my letter is gone?"

"Well, I got the mail, right? And I put it on the table in

the foyer. Then after I talked to you, I went back to get it, but it was gone."

"All the mail was *gone*?"

"Yes."

"So someone moved it," I say. "Go find it."

"Yeah, Mom moved it into the kitchen," he says. "But when I looked through the pile there, the letter wasn't in it."

I'm close to the ocean now, and water sloshes over my bare feet. It's pretty cold, but I don't even notice. A feeling of dread is taking over my body. "So just ask Mom where the letter is," I say. "And then tell her you're going to send it to me in Florida."

"She went back to work," he says. "And she's not answering her cell."

At that moment, someone taps me on the shoulder. I'm so on edge that I almost shriek out loud. I turn around, half expecting to see my mom standing there, holding the letter out to me with a disapproving look on her face, demanding answers and explanations.

But it's not my mom.

It's a guy I've never seen before. He looks a couple of years older than me, maybe nineteen or so, with dirty-blond hair. He's wearing a pair of navy-blue board shorts and a soft-looking gray T-shirt.

"Hey there," he says.

"Um, hi," I say.

He gives me a smile, revealing a row of perfect white teeth. "How are ya?"

"I'm fine."

"Who's that?" Neal demands.

"I'm not sure," I say. "Just some random guy on the beach."

"A random guy on the beach is hitting on you?" Neal asks. "I'll kill him."

"Are you here with the school trip?" the guy asks.

"Yes," I say, not sure if I should be admitting that. He looks like he's up to no good. He's probably friends with that vagrant who came by our room earlier and sold Paige and Celia beer. In fact, he might *be* the vagrant who came up to our room earlier and sold Paige and Celia beer.

"Sorry," I say. "I'm not interested in any beer."

"Beer?" the guy repeats, looking at me in shock. "At this time of day?"

"Yeah," I say. "Isn't that why you're here? To ask me if I want to buy beer?"

"You think I look like the type of guy who comes up to random underage girls and asks them if they want to buy beer?"

I think about the question. He actually *does* kind of look like that guy. He has that beach slacker thing going on, like maybe he spends his days surfing and his nights trolling the island for women. Not that he probably has any trouble finding women—he's very good-looking. Not my type, but still very good-looking. "Kind of," I say honestly.

"Wow, I'm offended," he says. But he doesn't seem offended. He's still smiling. He has a very nice smile. Very comforting. He probably uses it when he's out trolling for women. "What's your name?"

"Don't talk to him!" Neal instructs. "He's probably a murderer or a kidnapper. Like that guy who took Natalee Holloway."

"Lulubell," I say, because who gives their real name out to a random stranger? "What's yours?"

"Don. Don Donson."

"Don Donson?" I repeat. "Your name's Don Donson?"

"Sounds like a fake name!" Neal yells. "Stay away from him, Quinn."

"Yeah," he says, and shrugs. "What's wrong with that name?"

"It sounds made up."

"So does yours," he counters.

"That's because mine *is* made up."

"So is mine."

"You gave me a fake name?"

"So? You did, too."

I shake my head, wondering how the hell I got involved in a conversation with an obviously unstable person. "I'm sorry," I say. "But what is it that you wanted?"

"I wanted to invite you to a party we're having tonight at the club where I work." Aha! I knew I had him pegged—he *does* spend his days surfing and his nights working at some club where he trolls for women. He holds a hot-pink flyer out to me, and against my better judgment, I take it.

"A *party?*" Neal's asking. "Do not go to a *party* with him, Quinn. That's how girls go on class trips and come home statistics!"

"Thanks," I say to the guy standing in front of me. "I'll try to make it." Not.

His eyes meet mine, and a tiny little smile plays at the corner of his lips. He has nice lips, full but not so full they make him look feminine. In fact, he looks very manly—broad shoulders, chiseled jaw. The way he's looking at me makes me shiver. He doesn't say anything for a beat longer than necessary, then finally he says, "I hope you do."

And then he turns around and starts down the beach. For some reason I turn and watch him go, admiring how relaxed he looks, how easily he stops to give out flyers, talking to complete strangers like it's nothing. A girl in a red bikini takes a flyer from him, leaning in close to hear what he's saying. He smiles at her the same way he smiled at me, and I'm surprised to realize I'm a little jealous.

"Hello?" my brother yells. "Are you there or not?"

"Yes, I'm here." I shake my head and turn away from Fake Name Don. "Look," I say. "Are you going to be able to find the letter or not?"

"I just *told* you no. It's gone. Mom probably took it to work with her."

"Can you go down there and get it?" I ask desperately.

"To her work? No, I can't go down to her work. Why do you care if she has it anyway?"

Because if she reads it, she's going to find out I didn't get in! I can feel myself inching toward becoming hysterical, and so I do my best to make sure my voice stays calm. "Oh, I wouldn't say I *care* exactly. I just kind of wanted to open it myself."

"Are you sure that's all it is?" Neal asks suspiciously. "Because you're acting very strange."

For a second I think about telling him the truth. I mean, why not confide in my brother? He can be a good listener when he wants to be, and he knows all about bureaucracy and red tape—he's always starting letter-writing campaigns, and he's even interned in a bunch of state senators' offices.

"Quinn?" Neal asks. His voice has changed now, from one of annoyance to one of concern. "Seriously, is everything okay?"

I open my mouth to tell him. But then I stop. How can I? Neal wouldn't understand. He wouldn't understand, because Neal has gotten everything he's ever wanted. He got into Stanford. He made the varsity basketball team when he was in ninth grade. He was valedictorian of his class. In my family, if you work hard for something, you get it. And if you fail, it's not because you couldn't do it, it's because you haven't worked hard enough.

But I *have* worked hard. And I'm going to work harder. I'm not giving up. I'm going to wait and see what Genevieve has to say about my email before breaking down and telling my brother.

"Everything's fine," I say. "I just really wanted to open that letter myself."

"Okay," Neal says, but he doesn't sound sure. "Well, just send Mom a text and tell her that."

"I will."

"All right," he says. "Talk to you soon."

We hang up, and I send my mom a quick text, telling her that I heard my letter from Stanford arrived and I'm so excited, but can she please not open it because I want to do it myself, and can she maybe give it to Neal so that he can overnight it to me in Florida? I think about asking her to overnight it herself, but the less time she spends with that envelope, the better.

I'm on my way back to Celia and Paige when the text from my mom comes in.

I already opened it. Please call me.

# FIVE

CELIA IS DRUNK. OR AT LEAST, THE BEERS SHE had earlier combined with her time in the sun is making her feel sick. When she wakes up on the beach two hours later, she's nauseous and wants to go back to the room.

"I don't feel good," she moans to me as we walk her back toward our hotel.

"Yeah, me neither," I say. It's true. I haven't had anything to drink, but my stomach has been churning ever since I got that text from my mom. I haven't called her. I haven't heard back from Genevieve, either. The whole thing is making me feel like I'm going to throw up. Every time I swallow I can taste acid in the back of my mouth.

"How are we going to get her inside?" Paige asks.

I resist the urge to roll my eyes. Why is she asking *me* what to do? It's not my fault Celia got drunk. It's not really anyone's fault, I guess. Except Celia's. I mean, Paige and I aren't her keepers. Although Paige *was* with her when Celia bought the beer and then drank it.

"I don't know, Paige," I say. "We'll just have to do our best." I sniff the air around Celia. "She doesn't smell like beer or anything. If anyone asks, we'll just say she might have sun poisoning."

Luckily, when we get into the lobby of the hotel, it's empty. We start dragging Celia down the hall. "Ooh, I'm going to throw up," she says. She leans against the side of the wall and then slides all the way down until she collapses in a heap on the floor. Her legs are all askew, and her left boob is coming dangerously close to popping out of her bikini top.

"Gross," Paige says.

"Celia, honey, try to wait until we get to the room," I beg.

The last thing I want is to clean puke up off the floor. How disgusting.

We manage to get Celia to the room and into the bathroom before she loses the contents of her stomach.

"Gross," Paige says again as we stand outside the door, listening to Celia retch. I resist the urge to be annoyed with Paige because she's so useless.

Instead, I knock on the bathroom door. "Celia, sweetie, are you okay?"

"Yes," comes the faint reply.

"Do you want one of us to come in there?"

"No. I'm just going to rinse my mouth and then I'll be out." The sound of the toilet flushing comes through the door.

"She sounds better," I say to Paige. "She probably just needs to sleep some more."

Celia emerges from the bathroom, looking surprisingly put together, and drops onto the bed. "I need to sleep, just for a few," she says. A second later, a loud snore fills the room.

I have to get out of this room. I have to get out of this room so I can go make a plan. Plus, it's very claustrophobic in here—definitely not good for my stressed-out stomach. But what kind of excuse can I come up with to leave Paige here alone with Celia?

I give a big yawn. "Well, Celia seems fine now," I say brightly. "Maybe we should all take a nap. You know, in our own rooms."

Paige is sitting on her bed, sifting through this huge Ziploc bag of jewelry she brought. She pulls out a big tangle of necklaces and looks at them forlornly.

"Great," she says. "My necklaces are all screwed up." She sighs and starts trying to pick them apart with her fingers. I wonder why the hell she put them in a plastic bag if she didn't want them to get all tangled. Then I realize this is a horribly mean thought to have. I shouldn't take my bad mood out on Paige just because my life is a complete and total mess. It's not right.

"Can you help me?" she asks.

Sigh.

I take the tangle of metal chains out of her hand and start to pull at them. Wow. She really has gotten these all tangled up. At least they don't look that expensive. More like stuff she got at Express or Old Navy. Probably her parents made her leave her expensive jewelry at home.

"Thanks," Paige says, sounding relieved. "That was making me feel stressed."

"You know what you should do," I say kindly. "You should take a nap."

"But I'm not tired."

"Well, you don't have to sleep. You could just have some quiet time. You know, to relax and recharge. I can, too. You know, in my room." She's looking at me blankly, so I decide it's time to make it more clear. "I think I'm going to go back to my room now for a nap."

Paige glances over at Celia. "What about her?"

"I'm sure she's fine," I say. "She's just going to be sleeping. You can handle it."

A look of doubt crosses over Paige's face, and then her eyes flick down to the necklaces in my hands. "I think you're making it worse."

I look down and see that she's right. The chains are in an

even bigger tangle than they were when I started. "Oh," I say. "Um, well, this is one of those things that might have to get worse before it gets better. You know, like a staph infection."

"Staph infections don't get worse before they get better," Paige says. "And I don't think necklaces do, either."

Before I can refute what she's saying, my phone rings. My stomach drops into my shoes. My mom! It has to be! She's calling to find out why I haven't called her yet. I won't answer it. There's no way I can. I have to come up with a plan first, figure out what I'm going to do, what I'm going to say.

I really need to talk to Genevieve, so that by the time I talk to my mom, I'll be able to give her the good news that the whole letter was a mistake. Or maybe I'll tell her the truth— that the letter was actually true, but that I took matters into my own hands and made them reverse their decision. I can't decide which one is better—that I got accepted in the first place or that I made them change their minds. Honestly, probably that I got accepted in the first place.

Of course, that means I'll have to hope my mom won't find out I convinced my way in. But how would she ever find out? I'm going to be eighteen in a couple of months, and college acceptances are supposed to be personal and confidential. When Paige turned eighteen last month, the pharmacy stopped letting her mom pick up Paige's prescriptions until they got permission from Paige. Of course, Paige's mom already knew she was on birth control, because she's the one who took her to the gyno when she turned fifteen.

I reach over and pick up my phone, wincing as I look down at the caller ID.

Oh. It's not my mom.

It's a 941 area code, and the caller ID flashes UNKNOWN, SARASOTA, FL.

Is someone from the hotel calling me? Have they figured out we've smuggled in a drunk Celia and are now calling to let us know they're going to be notifying our parents and sending us home? Actually, now that I think about it, that wouldn't be the end of the world. If I got in trouble and was sent home, I could use it as an excuse for why I didn't get into Stanford.

I answer the phone and put on my most professional-sounding voice.

"Hello?"

"Hello, may I speak with Ms. Quinn Reynolds, please?" The voice on the other end is female and sounds young and very pleasant. If it was someone calling to bust us for drinking, I doubt she'd be so excited-sounding to talk to me. And I doubt she'd be so young. They'd probably leave it to some old person to yell at us.

"This is she," I say.

"Hi, Quinn, this is Margot Duvall from Biogene," she says.

I sit up straight on the bed. Margot Duvall is the woman who's supposed to be interviewing me for my internship! Things are looking up!

"Hello, Margot," I say smoothly. "It's lovely to speak with you."

"Who's Margot?" Paige stage-whispers. She frowns down at her necklaces and then brings one up to her mouth and begins working on a knot with her teeth.

I make a gesture at her to be quiet, and she rolls her eyes in a *sor-ry for living* kind of way.

"It's lovely to speak with you, too, Quinn," Margot Duvall says. She has that polished way of speaking you only get from going to boarding school in Connecticut. This isn't a guess—I know she went to boarding school in Connecticut because I know everything about her. Well, everything about her that's available on the internet. Anytime you're interviewing for a position, you should get to know everything you can, not only about the company, but about the person interviewing you.

"Anyway," Margot goes on. "I'm calling because we received your email, the one you sent yesterday?"

"Yes," I say. "I'm very eager to set up a time to come and meet you."

Margot Duvall sighs. "Yes, well, that's why I'm calling. I'm so sorry, Quinn, but I have to let you know that the internship has been filled. We found the perfect candidate, and she's accepted the position."

For a second, I have no idea what she's talking about. In fact, I feel like maybe I've misheard her. Did she just say they found the perfect candidate for the job? How is that possible? I'm the perfect candidate for the job!

Celia moans from the other side of the room, then leans over and clutches her stomach. "Ooh," she says. "I really don't feel good again." Then she pukes onto the rug.

"Oh, for god's sake," Paige says. She looks at me accusingly. "Why didn't you put a trash can down for her?"

"I'm sorry," Margot says from the other end of the line. "Is this a bad time?"

"No, it's a great time." I stand up and slip out the door of the room and into the hallway. Which, thankfully, is clear. I take a few steps toward the lobby so that Celia and Paige can't overhear me. "I'm sorry, so what was it you were saying?"

"I was saying that I'm sorry, but unfortunately, the internship position has been filled."

"But I don't understand," I say. "I've been trying to confirm a time for my interview for the past few days, and no one's gotten back to me."

"I know," she says, and her tone is a little more clipped this time, like it's lost some of its polish. "Because we've filled the position. So I'm sorry, but it's no longer available."

"But you promised me an interview." I'm shocked to

realize that *my* voice has lost some of its polish as well. How can this be happening? How can they have just offered the position to someone else? You can't just offer a position to someone else after you've promised someone else an interview. It's not polite. Or nice.

"I know, and I'm terribly sorry." I hear another line ringing in the background. "But at least now you'll get to enjoy your senior trip."

"But I don't want to enjoy my senior trip, I want to have an internship at your company!" Wow. I sound slightly hysterical. I wonder if maybe I didn't put on enough sunscreen. Sometimes when I sit in the sun for too long I start to get a little nutso. I try to compose myself. "What I mean is, um, are there any alternate opportunities you may feel I'm qualified for? A different internship, perhaps?"

"I'm sorry," Margot says, but she doesn't really sound sorry. She sounds actually like she's glad they gave the job to someone else and not a crazy person like me. "But we only have one position available for someone right out of high school."

I think about begging her, or asking if I can come for an interview anyway, but I know I need to get off the phone before I completely lose my dignity and any chance I have of working with her in the future. "I'm sorry to hear that," I say. "But if something comes up, please do keep me in mind."

"Of course."

We hang up and I just stand there for a moment, stunned. My phone buzzes and I look down at it, but it feels weird, like the hand holding my phone isn't even connected to my body.

One new email. I pull it up.

From Genevieve.

In the Stanford admissions office.

Dear Quinn,

Thank you so much for your email. Unfortunately, all decisions of the Stanford Admissions Committee are final and binding. We have a very strict process that ensures the merit of every applicant is taken into consideration. Since everything is done by committee, there is no appeals process as you inquired about.

Thank you so much for your interest in Stanford University.

~Genevieve Peletier

Wow. She definitely doesn't sound as nice as she did before. Probably she thinks I'm psycho. Am I psycho? I feel a little bit psycho. My heart is beating fast in my chest, and suddenly I can't breathe.

I try to calm myself down, but the hallway suddenly feels unbearably hot. Even though my face feels like it's burning, goose bumps break out on my arms. The floor starts to spin under my feet, and I know I need to get out of there.

I walk quickly through the lobby and out the double doors, then just keep walking until I get to the end of the cobblestone path. I push my way out onto the sand, onto the beach, and keep going until I reach the ocean. The cold water floods up onto my legs, and it must shock my system or something, because I immediately start to feel a little better.

I gulp in the salty air and try to get my heart rate to slow to normal, but it's not really working. It's pounding so hard I'm afraid that people around me are going to hear it, or at least notice that I'm freaking out.

I decide that maybe I need to sit down on the beach.

And that's when I see him.

Nathan Carson.

Lying on the sand a few feet away from me.

Making out with Gracie Noble. Their legs are tangled together, and his hands are in her hair. I just stand there for a second, watching them. And then I laugh, because it really is pretty comical. It's not even that I liked Nathan that much, not even that I wanted to hook up with him that badly.

It's just that in the span of a few hours, everything I had that was even a *possibility* is gone from my life. Stanford. Gone. My internship. Gone. Kissing Nathan. Gone. My parents being proud of me. Gone.

Gone, gone, gone, gone.

I want to scream out loud and kick the sand, which is strange, because I've never had anger issues. In fact, I've always thought anger was kind of a wasted emotion. Why waste time being angry about something when there's always something you can do to fix the situation?

But how am I supposed to fix this one? I didn't get into Stanford. It's the first time in my life that I've worked really hard for something and had it not pan out. Four whole years I worked for it. More, if you count all the time in middle school I put toward getting good grades so that I could qualify for all the advanced classes I took in high school.

It's making me really angry, thinking about it. Celia's upstairs, drunk and throwing up on the floor, and *she* gets to go to the school she's always wanted to go to. She gets everything she wants, pretty much, including any guy she wants. All she does is break rules and get rewarded for it! All I do is follow them, and everything goes to complete and total shit!

My phone buzzes then, and I look down at it, ready to take my rage out on whoever it was who would be stupid enough to call me at this exact moment. I'm almost halfway hoping that it's my mom. I'm in just the right mood to talk to her.

But it's not a phone call.

It's an email.

From me.

To me.

**Before graduation, I promise to . . .** *do something crazy.*

I blink at the screen.

A little frisson of anticipation runs up my spine. Why shouldn't I do something crazy? After all, playing by the rules hasn't gotten me anywhere.

# SIX

OF COURSE, *DECIDING* TO DO SOMETHING crazy and *actually doing* something crazy are two different things. I don't even know how to begin to go about it. I suppose I could go parasailing or something, but that seems kind of lame. I mean, yeah, I know parasailing is technically probably really dangerous, but your odds of dying from it aren't even that good, which definitely ruins some of the excitement.

And besides, parasailing isn't breaking the rules. And that's what it feels like I should do—something that's *not allowed*. I could always go out partying tonight with Celia and Paige and see what kind of trouble we could get into, but the thought of that kind of makes me want to poke my eyes out. I'd probably just end up following Celia around, making sure she doesn't have so much to drink that she can't walk. My role within our little group is to make sure Celia and Paige don't get into too much trouble—and tonight I want to *be* the troublemaking one.

I glance around the beach, looking for some crazy-making inspiration. And that's when a girl in a red-and-white-striped bikini walks by, holding a familiar-looking piece of hot-pink paper.

The guy on the beach. The one who told me his name was Don. The one who invited me to the club where he works. A club. On the beach. It sounds dangerous and forbidden. I'll go by myself, I decide. Not with Celia and Paige.

I'll dance. And do . . . whatever other things people do at clubs.

Once I've made the decision, I feel a lot better. About everything—Stanford, my parents, stupid Nathan. Everything just seems . . . like it's going to be okay somehow.

Now I just need to find a killer outfit.


Okay, so it definitely might be a tiny bit insane that I'm taking something so seemingly ridiculous to such an extreme level. I mean, obviously it's normal to be disappointed about not getting into Stanford. But to suddenly decide I want to throw caution to the wind and listen to a crazy email I sent myself when I was fourteen? Yeah, it's a little over the top.

On the other hand, anything can happen when you feel like your life's work has all been for nothing. I know I'm only seventeen. But going to Stanford is all I've ever wanted *in my life*. Seventeen years is a long time to want something. So it kind of makes sense that I'm spiraling.

When I walk into the lobby of the hotel, my head is spinning. But it's not the same kind of spinning it was doing before—before, I felt out of control, like I was losing my mind. Now I'm spinning in a good way, like something exciting is about to happen. It's the same feeling you get right before you go on a roller coaster. (Not that I've ever been on a roller coaster—who wants to vomit all over themselves or get stuck upside down or be involved in a fatal accident caused by faulty equipment? But if I ever had been on a roller coaster, this is how I imagine it would feel.)

I hesitate for a second at the elevator, wondering if I should go and check on Celia. But if I go to Paige and Celia's room, they're never going to let me leave. They're going to ask me a million questions until they break me down.

And I'm determined to do this. By myself.

I get in the elevator and push the button for the second floor.

Time to go back to my room and get ready to go to the club! What does one wear to a club? Definitely not what I'm wearing now, which is my bathing suit and cover-up. And definitely not the khaki shorts and tank tops I tend to wear in the summer. Do I have anything that's club appropriate?

Clubbing! I'm going clubbing!

As soon as I step off the elevator and onto my floor, a text comes in from Paige.

**Where'd u go?**

I hesitate for a second, then decide to avoid and deflect.

**Is Celia okay?**

**She's fine, she's sleeping.**

Pause.

**Where r u???**

**I don't feel so good—too much sun, I think—gonna head back to my room and nap for a bit.**

Wow. That lie slipped out of me like it was nothing. Of course, it's a temporary solution—a pretend nap isn't going to keep them from wondering where I am all night.

But whatever. I'll worry about Celia and Paige later. Planning things out hasn't gotten me anywhere. I mean, I tried to plan out my whole summer, my whole next year, my whole *future*, and look what happened. It all fell apart. So I think it's probably better to take this night moment by moment. As soon as I decide this, I feel almost giddy. I for sure could be having a mental breakdown.

When I open the door to my hotel room a few seconds later, Lyla's there, sitting cross-legged on her bed. Her presence throws me—I wasn't expecting anyone to be here. She looks up at me and our eyes meet, and in that second, I miss her so much I can hardly take it.

I suddenly wish the three of us were still friends, that

we were here on this trip together, that I wasn't stuck with Paige and Celia. If I were here with Lyla and Aven, I wouldn't have to pretend I didn't get into Stanford. Lyla and Aven don't care about stuff like that—if I'd told them I didn't get in, they'd understand. They'd help me come up with a way to tell my parents, they'd soothe me and tell me all about how Yale and Georgetown are completely amazing schools, they'd take me out to a club if that's what I wanted to do, even if they thought it was a dumb idea.

I hesitate for a second, then turn and walk into the bathroom without saying anything to Lyla. Then I turn around and come back out. If I'm going to be true to my whole not-planning-everything-out strategy, maybe I should try to talk to her. It's how I'm feeling in this moment.

I look at her, sitting there on the bed, and that same feeling of missing her overtakes me. It's so strong I feel my eyes fill with tears. The three of us were so close—not just friends. We were like sisters—so different, but when we were around each other, it didn't matter. I loved hanging out at Aven's house, cooking out on her grill, swimming in her pool. I loved going shopping with Lyla, waiting patiently while she'd take her time trying on fifteen different T-shirts before picking out the one she wanted.

I miss them both so much. I want to be friends again.

But when Lyla turns and looks at me, I lose my nerve. What could I possibly say to her that would change anything? How could I possibly even begin to apologize for what I did to her? Especially since she made it perfectly clear she doesn't want to hear what I have to say.

Now that I'm out here, though, I can't just turn around and go back into the bathroom without saying anything. I'll look like a total idiot.

"Please tell me you didn't use all the hot water," is what I come up with. It's a completely ridiculous thing to say—why the hell would I think she used up all the hot water? Can you even use up all the hot water at a hotel? I'm pretty sure they have, like, an unlimited supply.

"I didn't use all the hot water," she says, all snotty-like. "I've been out of the shower for at least an hour."

"Right," I mutter, mostly because I don't want her to think I care. I walk back into the bathroom and shut the door and then I just stand there for a moment, wondering if I should go back out there. I want to tell her about Stanford, I want to ask her what she's been up to, I want to ask her what happened between her and her mom and her dad after I did what I did. I want to order room service with her and forget about this whole plan of going out clubbing. I want to stay here with Lyla and Aven.

*That's never going to happen,* a voice in my head whispers. *She hates you. And she* should *hate you. What you did to her was unforgivable, and this is your punishment—you lost her friendship.*

So I do what I do every time I think about Lyla—I tell

myself it's not all my fault. I apologized to her. I did every-thing I could. And she just blew me off, like it was nothing. She just shut down. And that wasn't right.

Whatever.

I'm done with letting my past derail me. I need to focus on the present. And the present right now is sticking to my plan.

My phone buzzes again with my email.

Before graduation, I promise to . . . *do something crazy.*

Don't worry, universe . . . I'm coming for you.


After my shower, it's time to work on my clubbing look. There's a tangle of makeup sitting on the counter, stuff Aven and Lyla must have left out. I pull my own makeup bag out from where I stashed it under the counter, survey all the stuff in front of me, and then get to work—smoky metallic shadow on my eyes, two coats of mascara, and tons of big, springy curls in my hair.

I usually make it a rule not to wear much makeup—why waste time putting a bunch of crap on your face that's just going to make you break out? But I'm actually pretty good with makeup, because I've watched Celia and Paige getting ready, like, five bazillion times.

Now I just have to worry about my outfit.

My carry-on bag is sitting in the corner of the bathroom

where I left it. I wanted to unpack it, but my laptop is in there, and I didn't know who was going to be coming in and out of our room. Who knows who Aven and Lyla might be hanging out with these days—there could be all sorts of nefarious characters in their social circles, just looking for a laptop to steal.

But now I remember I put a few clothes in my carry-on, too—just in case something happened to my luggage, I didn't want to be stuck in Florida with nothing to wear. I rummage through it now, wondering if there's anything in there that's club appropriate.

I come up with a white tank top and a gauzy white shirt, along with a red-and-white-striped halter. Both of the shirts— the white tank and the halter—are supposed to be worn underneath the gauzy shirt. But I can't wear a gauzy shirt to a club. Even I know that would be completely ridiculous.

I pull the tank top on and study my reflection in the mirror. It's kind of tight and low-cut, and without the gauzy shirt over it, it could work. And then I remember something. The red-and-white-striped halter—when I first bought it, Celia laughed and said it was one of those shirts girls like Katie Wells would wear as a skirt. Which at the time I thought was totally ridiculous, because hello, the shirt would be way too short as a skirt. (Also, it wasn't that nice of Celia to make fun of Katie Wells, because Celia and Paige wore skirts just as short all the time. But Celia was pissed because Katie had just gotten Most Attractive in the class superlatives poll, and even though Celia got Best Smile, I think she was secretly hoping to get the Most Attractive award instead.)

Anyway, at the time I didn't think anything about it—it was just a throwaway comment. But now I wonder if I could use the halter as a skirt. I step into it and pull it up over my hips, feeling ridiculous. It's obscenely short, and my hands immediately go back to my waist to take it off. I'm already venturing way out of my comfort zone to go to a club—I can't wear this in public.

But then I stop. Why can't I? Girls dress like this all the time. And not just girls like Katie Wells, but girls like Celia and Lyla and even Aven. At least, she did once. The three of us went to a Halloween party sophomore year, and Aven went as a sexy cat. Which basically meant wearing a black ballerina skirt and a black bodysuit and then painting her face to look like a cat. She thought Liam would like it if she showed her sexier side. Of course, he ended up making out with some girl from another school all night, and so Aven's outfit was for nothing. But still. The point is she *wore* it.

Just because I'm not used to dressing like this doesn't mean I *shouldn't*. It's like colleges are always saying—they don't need the smartest candidates or even the best ones—they need the most well-rounded. New experiences are always a good thing. So before I can change my mind, I turn and walk out of the bathroom.

Lyla's lying on her bed, a faraway look on her face, like she's deep in thought about something. Why is she spending her vacation in this room? Doesn't she want to be out and about, getting into mischief, like me?

"Why the hell didn't I pack that bustier?" she mutters.

Which makes no sense. Why the hell would she pack a bustier on vacation to Florida? It's, like, eighty-five degrees and humid every single day. She'd be sweating like crazy.

"Wow," I say. "Sounds like a personal problem."

She turns her gaze toward me, and I see her eyes widen as she takes in my outfit. "What the hell are you wearing?" she blurts.

"Seriously?" I ask her. "You're wishing for a bustier and you're questioning *my* fashion choices?" I mean, come on. I pull a lipstick out of my purse, then paint my lips with it and drop it back in my purse. Wow. This lipstick is a little . . . bold. But that's okay. I'm in a bold kind of mood.

"Um," Lyla says. "Is everything okay?"

Well, let's see. I didn't get into Stanford, I'm about to go out to a club by myself in a strange place wearing a shirt as a skirt, and I'm avoiding my mother because she's probably going to disown me. "Everything's fine," I say. "Why do you ask?" I pull out some perfume and spritz it all over my body. It was a birthday present from my aunt, and I totally forgot I even had it in my purse. Usually I don't wear perfume—another thing that seems like a complete waste of time.

"Since when did you start wearing perfume?" Lyla asks, which totally annoys me. It's like, now you want to pretend that you're interested in my life? After you've been blowing me off for years and years? Well, two years. But still.

"Since, like, forever," I lie.

"Are you sure you're okay?" she asks again. And her tone sounds so sincere that for a moment, I think about telling her what happened. I think about telling her that I didn't get into Stanford, that I didn't get my internship, that Nathan was on the beach kissing some girl, and even though I don't like him that much, it somehow made me upset.

But instead I just say, "Don't wait up!" in this totally fake cheerful voice, and then I turn around and walk out the door.

I'm almost safely out of the lobby when I spot Celia and Paige.

They're sitting in the big leather chairs by the front door. Celia is sipping coffee, and Paige is looking at something on her phone.

Shit, shit, shit. How am I going to slip out to party at some club with the two of them sitting right there? And

what are they doing down here anyway? Celia was just puk-
ing not that long ago. Does she really think a cup of coffee
is going to fix her up? Actually, she looks remarkably put
together for someone who just had a spell.

I start to head back down the hall—there's got to be
another door out of this place—when Paige sees me.

"Quinn?" she asks, confused.

I look around and blink rapidly, like I'm surprised to
see them here. Then I try to act pleased. "Oh, um, hi! I was
just back at your room looking for you, but you guys weren't
there. You know, obviously. Because you're down here now."
The lie rolls off my tongue quite easily, and it's actually brilliant. It makes it seem like I was looking for them when I
really wasn't. Who knew I was so good at thinking on my
feet? Now if only I could come up with some plausible excuse
for why I didn't get into Stanford.

"You look amazing!" Celia says. She stands up quickly.
"I feel better," she says. She looks a lot better—the color
is back in her face, and her eyes are bright. "I just needed
to get it out of my system." I'm not sure if she means the
need to party, or all the alcohol she drank. Either way it's a
bit disturbing. She motions to the coffee table, which has
a bunch of greasy paper plates scattered on it, along with
some pizza crusts. "Plus, I ate pizza, and you know that
soaks up alcohol."

That makes no sense and is actually kind of gross—picturing a bunch of pizza soaking up the alcohol in her stomach. I want to tell her there was probably nothing left to soak up because she threw it all up, but she just keeps talking. "So what are we doing tonight? Obviously you seem like you're ready to parrrty." She takes my hand and twirls around the lobby, then giggles as she almost falls over. "Oops," she says. "Not ready for that."

I think about lying and saying I was going to just spend the night hanging out on the beach or that I don't feel good and want to finish my nap. But there's no way they're going to buy that—not when I'm dressed like this. Maybe I should just nix my entire plan and go to whatever lame party the two of them are planning to go to tonight. I can sip on a warm wine cooler in the corner of some hotel room and then take care of Celia when she gets drunk.

But what would be the point? It's just going to leave me completely depressed, and then tomorrow I'm going to wake up and everything's going to be exactly the same. I'm going to be here, in Florida, avoiding my mom, with no internship and no Stanford.

*Before graduation, I promise to . . . do something crazy.*

I want to do it. I want to do something crazy.

So I pull the wrinkled flyer about the party out of my purse and show it to Celia. "I want to go to this," I say.

She studies the paper, then looks up at me, her eyes wide.

"This looks awesome," she says. "What has gotten into you, Quinn Reynolds?"

"I don't know," I say, shaking my head. "I guess I'm just ready for a change."

# SEVEN

AN HOUR LATER—PAIGE AND CELIA HAD TO get ready—we're walking down the strip to the Ocean Club. It's a lame name for a club, but I'm hoping the inside is going to be more fun than the name implies.

"Now listen," Celia says, "when we get in there, make sure to flirt with some of the college guys, the ones who are over twenty-one." She tilts her head and thinks about it. "But no guys who are too good-looking—focus on the ones who are nice but a little homely. Like a Seth Rogen type. That way they'll buy us drinks. You know, because they're desperate."

There's so much wrong with this statement that I don't even know where to begin. I resist the urge to point out that Seth Rogen is actually really cute and has a hot wife and is, like, a gazillionaire who's super successful and smart. Also, why should we make guys think they're going to get to hook up with us so they'll buy us alcohol? That seems almost as skeezy as the guys plying us with drinks because they think they might get lucky.

I look over to Paige so we can share a secret eye roll, but she just nods at Celia and keeps walking.

I sigh, wondering again how the hell I'm friends with these two. But when we get to the club, I'm actually glad I have them with me. Something about being alone outside a club is a little scary. I've never been to a club before. I've only seen them on TV.

The bouncer checks our IDs—it's a seventeen-and-over club, but the people who are over twenty-one are getting blue ink stamps on their hands. For a moment, Celia gives the bouncer a big smile, the smile I've seen her give when she's trying to get something from someone. But he gives her a *don't even think about it* look.

Inside, the club is dark, and it takes a few minutes for my eyes to adjust. As soon as they do, I start to relax. This isn't the kind of club you see on TV, the kind that's seedy and scary-looking, with leather couches and tons of people dancing and grinding on each other.

In fact, it's sort of the opposite. There's an oval-shaped bar in the middle of the dance floor, and electric-blue lights in the shape of palm trees are draped lazily across the ceiling. Almost every seat at the bar is full, and there are a lot of people on the dance floor, but it's not super crowded yet.

Plus, you have to step down into that section—the part where we're standing has a bunch of high-tops scattered around a few pool tables.

"Let's a get a table and some sodas," I suggest. Now that I'm here, I'm actually a little disappointed. I'm starting to realize that going to a club isn't really all that crazy. Yes, it's put me out of my comfort zone, but now what? Do I dance? Get drunk? It all seems so uninteresting.

"Okay," Celia says. "But I don't want to waste too much time just sitting." Her eyes are scanning the room, looking for a mark.

"Him, him, him!" Paige screeches, grabbing at Celia's arm. "That one!" She points to a paunchy-looking guy sitting at a table with a couple of his buddies.

Celia looks over at Paige and gives her an admiring look. "Good job, Paige," she says. "Couldn't have done it better myself."

Paige beams.

I wait at the table while the two of them go and order us some Diet Cokes. But as soon as they return with our drinks, they decide they need something stronger.

"Diet Coke is for wimps," Paige whines.

"It totally is," Celia says. She eyes the guys over in the corner again. "Come on, let's go get them to buy us some drinks."

Paige jumps up happily.

"I think I'll just wait here," I say. "We don't want anyone to take our table." It's a totally useless thing to say—there aren't enough people here to take our table. But flirting with college guys to try to get them to buy us drinks doesn't sound fun. At all.

"Fine," Celia says, sounding annoyed. "But just so you know, if we can't get drinks here, we should go back to the hotel. There are, like, a million parties going on, and they're all going to have alcohol."

She gives me a look, like I'm the one who should be blamed for dragging her out here when I'm not even the one who wanted her to come.

I sigh and watch as the two of them saunter over to the table of guys and then sit down and introduce themselves.

Right on cue, my phone buzzes with my email again.

**Before graduation, I promise to . . .** *do something crazy.*

Yeah, but *what?* Sitting here at this table while Paige and Celia flirt with average-looking college boys so they can score drinks is actually really pathetic.

What was I thinking, coming here? I'm not the kind of girl who gets dressed up and goes out and mingles and dances. I should be at home, in bed, doing homework or applying for new internships. But the only reason I would be doing any of that was to make sure I got into Stanford. Now that I'm not getting into Stanford, homework and internships and extracurriculars seem totally pointless. My whole *life* seems completely pointless. I'm just about to get up and walk out the door and back to the hotel when someone breathes into my ear.

"Fancy seeing you here." The voice is deep and warm, and slightly familiar. The hairs on the back of my neck stand up, and a delicious warmth fills my belly.

I turn around.

The owner of the voice grins. "Hey, Tiffany."

It's him.

The guy from the beach.

"What's new?" he asks, and sits down in the seat next to me, like we're old friends who haven't seen each other in a while instead of strangers who just met this morning.

"Oh, you know," I say, taking a sip of my drink and trying to sound nonchalant. "Same old, same old. Avoiding the paparazzi, working on million-dollar mergers." It's supposed to sound like a joke, but it comes out sounding a little forced and weird.

"So nothing really new since this morning then," he says conversationally.

"Nope, nothing really new."

I fiddle with my drink and then finally look up at him. He looks like he knows he's making me uncomfortable and that he's actually enjoying it.

"Are you here by yourself?" he asks.

"Oh, no," I say quickly, not wanting him to think I came

here just to see him. "I'm with my two friends." I point to Paige and Celia over in the corner. As I do, Celia throws her head back, laughing at something one of the guys she's with is saying.

"They're trying to scam drinks, huh?" he asks.

"Yup," I say, before realizing it might not be the best idea to admit that. If he works here, then should I really be telling him that my underage friends are trying to get guys to buy them alcohol? What if he kicks them out? Or worse, calls the police? "I mean, sodas. They're trying to scam sodas."

"Right." He leans back in the chair, balancing it on its back legs in a way that looks really dangerous. But he doesn't seem nervous about falling. In fact, just the opposite. He seems totally relaxed and in control. His fingertips tap the high-top to the beat of the music.

"So what's your real name?" I ask, because I need to say something, otherwise it's just him sitting across from me, looking at me in that very disconcerting (albeit sexy) way.

"You tell me first," he says.

"Quinn."

He grins. "That's a really pretty name."

No guy has ever called my name pretty before. No guy has ever called anything about me pretty before. Not that I don't think I'm attractive. I mean, I'm not unattractive. I don't think. But I'm not what you'd consider sexy or anything like that. I have dark hair and I love my blue eyes, but my features are tiny and kind of delicate, which makes me cute. I'm not gorgeous or hot or any of the other kinds of things that make guys my age get all excited, like they do with Celia and her big hair and her big boobs.

He puts his chair down, then leans across the table. "How come you're not over there with your friends?"

I shake my head. "I don't drink."

"So?"

"So why would I go over there and try to get drinks from those guys?"

"I thought you said they were getting Cokes." He sits up and pushes his shoulders back. "Now that you've told me that, I'm going to have to report them."

"Um, I wasn't—"

He grins. "Relax, Quinn. I was just kidding. I don't care what your friends do. But seriously, how come you're over here all by yourself?"

I shake my head. "No way. Tell me your name first."

"Abram."

"Is that for real?"

He smiles. "Yeah. Now tell me why you're over here all by yourself."

"I don't know." I sigh. "I guess maybe I just wanted a break from them."

"From your friends?"

"Yeah." We both turn and look over to where Celia

and Paige are sitting. The waitress brings over a round of drinks and sets them down on their table, and as soon as she's gone, Paige climbs into the lap of a guy with a soul patch on his chin.

"Yeah," Abram says, "they definitely seem like the type of girls you'd need a break from." I like that he can recognize that just from seeing the way the two of them are acting. Maybe I should be upset that he's judging them, but it's the opposite—I'm glad someone's actually forming an opinion about Celia and Paige based on how they act, instead of how they look.

I'm finished with my drink, and I run my hand over the rim of the glass, my finger getting cold from the condensation. "So what about you?" I ask. "Shouldn't you be working?"

"I'm promotions," he says. "So all I have to do is get people in the door. I hand out flyers on the beach all day, then hope that I'm charming enough to get everyone to show up." He grins at me. "Obviously, I'm good at my job."

"I didn't come here because of you!" I protest.

"Okay." He shrugs, like it doesn't matter to him if I did or not.

"I didn't!"

"I said okay."

"But you said it like you don't believe me."

He shrugs again.

"So then why are you here?" I ask. "I mean, if you don't have to work. Did you come just to hang out and party?"

"No," he says. "I was looking for you."

I look up from the melting ice in my drink, expecting to see that same flirtatious gaze he was staring at me with earlier. But to my surprise, he looks completely serious.

"Yeah, right," I say, rolling my eyes. But my heart is beating strong in my chest, hoping he's telling the truth.

"No, seriously. I really was hoping you'd come."

"Okay." I'm not sure what to say to that. He has to be lying, right? I mean, he doesn't know anything about me. All he knows is that he met me on the beach, he gave me a flyer, and I showed up here. I'm not stupid enough to think I'm the first girl he's claimed to be waiting for. It's probably his mode of operation, what he does to get innocent tourists to sleep with him.

The club is getting busier now, and Abram looks at the people streaming through the door and nods in satisfaction, like he's responsible for it. Which I guess he is.

But then he turns to me. "Do you want to get out of here?"

"What?"

"Do you want to leave?"

"With you?"

"Yes, with me."

"I don't . . . I mean, I'm with my friends."

He looks back over to where Celia and Paige are sitting. We watch as one of the schlubbier-looking guys slides shots across the table. Celia and Paige pound them down, and everyone in their group cheers. Celia and Paige roll their eyes at each other when they think no one's looking, like they can't believe they have to do shots with such losers just to get drunk.

"Yeah," Abram says sarcastically. "They seem really concerned about you."

"I can't *leave* with you," I say. "I just met you, like, five seconds ago." I mean, how stupid could I be? Leaving a club with some guy I know nothing about? That's insane. It's how people end up disappearing and/or chopped up into a million pieces, just like my brother said.

"Five hours."

"What?"

"We met five hours ago. On the beach." He looks at his watch. I like that he's wearing a watch—it's one of those sports ones, the kind that's waterproof, and something about it is ridiculously sexy. "Actually, it's probably been seven or eight hours by now."

"Still," I say. "Knowing someone for seven or eight hours isn't enough to justify leaving a club with them."

"Isn't it?" He reaches out and grabs the pepper shaker

off the table and starts sliding it back and forth between his hands. The whole time his eyes are on mine, waiting for me to decide.

"I can't just leave with you," I say again. "I don't know anything about you."

"You know my name. And where I work."

"But that's all."

"True," he says seriously. He cocks his head and pretends to think about it. "I think you're right. It wouldn't really make sense for us to hang out. Since I'm a stranger and everything."

"It *wouldn't* make sense," I say. "It wouldn't be *smart*." I resist the urge to list all the reasons it's a bad idea, because I don't want to insult him by implying he could be a psycho murderer. Besides, it's really not something that needs to be explained. Is he used to girls just going home with him? He doesn't seem surprised I don't want to leave with him. But he doesn't seem particularly upset about it, either. Does he figure that if I turn him down he'll just find someone else to take home? I'm vaguely repulsed, but also slightly excited, like I'm going to miss my chance. Which is awful and against any kind of feminism, like, ever.

And then I remember that stupid email.

Before graduation, I promise to . . . *do something crazy*.

Yes, something crazy. But not something *dangerous*. Or worse, something dangerous like going home with a guy I just met. Something dangerous like going home with a guy I just met while on vacation in a strange place. He's cute, yes. And he seems harmless enough, albeit cocky. But still . . .

*Don't overanalyze it. How are you feeling—what do you want to do?*

I take in a deep breath.

And then, before I can change my mind, I turn and look at him.

"Okay," I say. "Let's get out of here."

# EIGHT

I CANNOT BELIEVE I'M DOING THIS. THIS IS insane. This is crazy. It's so much not like me that it's kind of astounding. But I'm starting to like the way it feels—it's like trying on a dress that's not really your style, then realizing it suits you after all.

"Should we go get something to eat first?" I ask as soon as we're out of the club. My stomach is flipping on itself, over and over again.

"First?" Abram stops on the sidewalk outside the club, and when he looks at me, I have to catch my breath at how absolutely gorgeous he is. Dirty-blond hair, a chiseled jaw, dark-green eyes, smooth tan skin. He's wearing an emerald-green T-shirt that reveals lean biceps and strong forearms. His cargo shorts hug his hips in a way that makes me think the rest of his body is just as perfect as the little I can see of it.

"Yes." I swallow and jut my chin out, daring him to tell me he won't take me to eat.

"First before what?"

"First before . . ." We hook up? You have your way with me? I'm not exactly sure how this whole thing works. I'm woefully inexperienced when it comes to the opposite sex. It's because I overthink everything. The last and only time I ever hooked up with a guy, it took me so long to decide if I actually wanted to do it (it involved multiple pros and cons lists), that it turned out to be kind of awful, mostly because by the time it happened, the guy wasn't even really that interested in me anymore.

The side of Abram's mouth slides up into a grin. "That's awfully presumptuous of you," he says.

"What is?"

"Thinking I was asking you to leave so that we could hook up."

"Well, weren't you?"

"Wasn't I what?"

"Hoping we were going to hook up."

He looks me up and down, his eyes lingering over my body, almost like he's deciding what to do with me. But it's not in a lecherous, gross kind of way. It's more like he's amused. "Were *you?*" he asks.

"Was I what?"

"Hoping we were going to hook up."

"No," I say, even though I obviously kind of was. Otherwise, what's the point of leaving with him? Going out to eat with a stranger is a lot less exciting than going to make out somewhere.

"Then let's go eat."

"Okay," I say, equal parts disappointed and relieved. A nice warm breeze hits my skin as I start to follow Abram down the main street of the key. The vibe outside has changed from when I was on the beach earlier—there are still plenty of kids and families, but now instead of wearing swimsuits and carrying inner tubes, they're dressed in khaki shirts and polo shirts, their hair damp from the shower, their faces red from a day in the sun.

Abram heads for a restaurant a few blocks down on the corner, called Hub Baja Grill, and leads me right up to the hostess stand.

"Hey, Jenna," he says to the girl working there. She has gorgeous long blond hair, and she's wearing a white, empire-waist maxi-dress with a twisty gold belt.

"Hey, Abram." She smiles. "Your usual table?"

"Perfect."

She leads us to an outside table that's situated with a view of the street, just far enough away from the guy playing banjo in the corner so that we can enjoy the music without it being so loud we can't talk. Jenna sets menus down in front of us and then turns and heads back toward the host-ess stand. I watch as she goes, admiring the way her long blond hair is pulled back in a loose braid. She has the whole casual, sexy beach look down perfectly. I wonder if Abram knows her just from coming here, or if she's one of his many conquests.

"So you're a regular here?" I ask.

Abram shrugs. He's leaning forward in his chair, so close that his knee brushes against mine under the table. Our bare skin touches, and I flush. His skin is warm, and his legs feel strong. "I'm kind of a regular everywhere."

"What do you mean?" I open the menu. It's on the small side, but everything looks amazing and very islandy—fresh-sounding seafood dishes, nachos with homemade guacamole and mango salsa, organic strawberry margaritas, and a yummy-looking tropical fruit salad.

"Just that I grew up on the island," Abram says. "So everyone kind of knows me."

"Especially pretty hostesses," I say before I can stop myself.

"Jenna?" He smiles. "You're jealous of Jenna?"

"No," I say haughtily. "I'm not jealous of anyone." The truth is, I am kind of jealous of her. Not because of anything she's done, or even because I think she's that pretty (which I do), but because she has a familiarity with Abram. Which is so stupid—why should I be jealous of her knowing Abram better than I do? I should be happy I don't know Abram that well. It makes hooking up with him more of a crazy thing to do.

Although are we even going to hook up now? Did I ruin my chance by insisting he take me out to dinner first? Am I overthinking everything? Why am I overthinking everything? *Just relax, Quinn. You're breezy. You're in the moment. You're winging it.*

"Good," Abram says, "because there's no reason to be jealous of Jenna. I've known her since I was a little kid. She's like my sister."

"Good," I say. "Because I'm not. Jealous, I mean."

"Good."

"Good." I turn back to the menu, wondering what I should order. I'm starving—by the time I stumbled on Paige and Celia in the lobby, the pizza they'd ordered was long gone, and so I haven't had any dinner. My stomach grumbles quietly in anticipation. Luckily, the music is loud enough that Abram doesn't hear.

"Aren't you going to look at the menu?" I ask.

"Nah. I already know what I want—dip sampler, teriyaki wings, honey-glazed salmon." He ticks them off on his fingers.

"That's a lot of food."

He smiles. "Yeah, well, it's been a long day." He raises his eyebrows at me, like he's thinking there's a chance it could be a long night, too.

But before I can figure out how to respond, a waitress appears at our table. Abram orders his plethora of food, and I go with the chicken quesadilla and the barbecue bacon cheeseburger.

"Impressive," Abram says, once the waitress is gone.

"What is?"

"Well, it's just that most girls try to pretend they don't eat. So they order a salad. Or, if they do actually order some food, they'll go with lobster, just because they're in Florida."

"I don't like lobster," I say, wrinkling my nose. "And if I did, I certainly wouldn't come all the way to Florida for it. I'd go to Maine, which is way closer to my house."

Abram laughs. "I like a girl who knows her seafood," he says. "And who doesn't care what people think." He inches his chair closer to mine.

"Do the girls you date usually care about what people think?"

"Enough not to order red meat."

I look him right in the eye. "Then I think you've been dating the wrong girls."

He cocks his head, like he's thinking about it. "Fair enough," he says. "So tell me about Quinn."

I frown. "Tell you about Quinn?"

"Yeah."

"Why are you referring to me in the third person?"

"Because I read somewhere that people find it less threatening."

"You think I find you threatening?"

"Don't you?"

"No."

"Intimidating?"

"No." Lie. Anyone as good-looking as Abram is going to be intimidating.

"Charming?" He leans in close on that last one, like he's really interested in the answer. My heart pounds in my chest.

"No." I shake my head emphatically.

"Liar."

"I'm not lying."

"But you came out to dinner with me."

"So?"

"So that must mean you find me at least a little charming."

"No. It just means that the club was boring."

"So you find me interesting, then."

"No."

"Lie."

"Seriously. If I found you interesting, do you think I would have ordered an appetizer and a cheeseburger? I would have ordered the side salad and the Florida lobster, which would have soured me on lobster forever, because obviously it wouldn't be as good as the ones from Maine."

He laughs, and I can tell he likes the fact that I can hold my own with this verbal sparring that we're doing. "Besides," I say mock seriously. "You shouldn't call a girl a liar. It's not nice."

"I didn't say you were a liar. I said you told a lie."

"Semantics." Are we flirting? I think we're definitely flirting. And the thing is, I'm pretty sure I'm good at it. Or at least, *he* thinks I am. The whole time we've been talking, he's been inching his chair closer to mine. He reaches out now and puts his hand on my knee, and fire slides up my thigh and into my belly.

And that's when someone starts screaming my name from down the street.

"Quinn!" The high-pitched shrieking is followed by the sound of heels clacking against the sidewalk. I turn to see Celia and Paige running toward us, their purses bouncing behind them. "Quinn!" Celia screeches. "Oh my goodness, Paige, there she is!"

"I see her," Paige grumbles. "Can we slow down now? These shoes are really hurting my feet."

"Where the hell have you been?" Celia demands, stopping on the other side of the railing that separates the seating area of the restaurant from the street. "We were looking all over for you." She turns her eyes to Abram, and a look flickers over her face—surprise, followed by interest. "Oh," she trills. "I didn't know you were with someone."

"Yeah," Paige pipes up. "We didn't know you were with someone." She drops her purse onto the sidewalk, then reaches down and unbuckles her gladiator sandal and begins massaging her ankle.

"Well, I am," I say cheerfully. "And I'm fine." Crap, crap, crap. I meant to text the two of them once I was out of the club and out of their line of sight—the last thing I wanted was them trying to convince me not to leave with Abram. But I totally forgot.

I'm glad they were worried enough about me to leave the club to come and find me, but honestly, I just want the two of them to go away. "Why didn't you just text me if you were so worried?"

"We tried to," Paige says. "But you weren't answering your phone."

I reach into my bag and pull out my cell. Oh. Five new texts, all from Paige and Celia, all along the lines of *where are you* or *where did you go* or *we're worried about you*. I can't believe they actually noticed I was gone.

"I didn't hear my phone," I say. Damn. Why, why, why didn't I text them and tell them I was okay, that I didn't feel good, that I was leaving and going back to my room? Then they wouldn't have followed me out here. Although I guess they didn't technically *follow* me. They were just looking for me. But still. I want them to leave. "I'm sorry I made you guys worry," I say. "But I'm fine, so . . ." I give Celia a pointed look, the kind of look that any normal person would know means, *Go away, I'm with a guy I maybe like and should be left to my own devices.*

But instead of doing any of those things, Celia leans over the railing so that the top of her shirt flutters down in the front. "I'm Celia," she says breathily.

"Abram," he says, taking her hand. Surprisingly, he doesn't take the opportunity to look down her shirt. I don't think I've ever seen a guy not want to look down Celia's shirt. "Thanks for coming to check up on Quinn. That was really nice of you."

Celia looks momentarily confused by his lack of interest in her breasts, but she recovers quickly. "Of course," she says, straightening up. "We would never let Quinn just run off by herself." She narrows her eyes at me. "Especially with a random boy."

"Oh, I'm not random," Abram says happily. "Quinn and I know each other."

"You do?" Celia frowns.

"Celia, can we go now?" Paige whines. "I'm starting to get a blister on my ankle."

"Yeah, we met on the beach earlier," I say breezily, like meeting someone on the beach is totally normal, and that if you do, you can leave clubs with them and not have to worry about them spiking your drink and/or killing you.

"When?" Celia demands. "Where was I?"

"I think you were getting sloppy drunk," I say. Wow. That came out of nowhere. Celia's mouth drops. Mine almost drops, too. I've never said anything like that to Celia before. I'm starting to kind of frighten myself. "No, but seriously, you guys," I say quickly, trying to gloss over the comment, "I'm fine. I swear."

The waitress returns and sets our food down in front of us.

"I'm going to have dinner with Abram, and then I'll text you." I make sure my voice sounds firm.

"No." Celia shakes her head. "No way. I'm not just leaving you here with some random."

"Celia," Abram says, pretending to be upset, "I'm starting to get a little offended at the fact that you keep calling me a random. It's not nice."

"Well, if you're not random, then you're strange," Celia insists. "And I can't just leave my friend with you." I want to point out that she's left me plenty of times, like at Bronx Crocker's eighteenth birthday party last month, when she decided to hook up with Jeremiah Brown and left me to find my own ride home. I had to call Neal to come get me at, like, two in the morning, and he definitely wasn't happy.

"Look, I'll tell you what," Abram says. He reaches across the railing and takes Celia's phone out of her hand. He dials his own phone, then picks up the call and ends it. "Now you have my phone number."

"Ha!" Celia says. "You can't just give me your phone number and expect me to be okay with it. You could be a serial murderer, and that could be a TracFone."

Wow. Celia's been watching way too many of those crime shows on A&E. I'm touched that she's doing her due diligence, though. I like the fact that someone's putting Abram on the spot, making him prove he's not dangerous. It's going to make it a lot easier to hook up with him later if I know he doesn't want to kill me.

Abram reaches into his pocket, pulls out his wallet, and slides his license onto the table. He snaps a pic of it with his phone, then texts it to Celia, using the number he got off his caller ID.

"Now you have a pic of my license," he says. "You have my phone number, my name, my address, my date of birth . . . actually, I should be more afraid of you than you are of me. You could steal my identity."

"Quinn doesn't want to stay here with you," Celia says. "She wants to leave with us!" She turns to Paige, who straightens back up and almost falls over trying to put her shoe back on. "Right, Paige?"

"Right," Paige says automatically, because it's what she's been trained to do. It's a programmed response, like when you ask Siri what the weather is like.

"No, I don't," I say. "I just told you I want to stay here."

Celia looks at me, suspicious. "Are you sure?"

"Yes, I'm sure."

She glances around wildly, like maybe she can find something she can use to make me go with her. "Okay," she says finally, but she doesn't move. "I guess . . . you'll call me later?"

"Sure."

"Okay. We can meet back up." Celia turns to Abram, then holds her phone up and waves it in the air. "I've got my eye on you." She grabs Paige's hand and pulls her down the sidewalk.

"Wow," Abram says once they're out of earshot. "Your friends are intense. But it's good they're looking out for you." He grabs one of the chips out of the sampler we've been served and dips into the little pot of salsa.

"I guess," I say. "I mean, they're over the top, but they mean well."

"Ahh," he says knowingly. "They're those kind of friends, huh?"

"What kind of friends?" I pick up a quesadilla and take a bite. I have to stop myself from moaning in pleasure. I wonder how anyone who lives here can keep themselves from weighing four hundred pounds. Maybe they can't. Maybe all the people I saw on the beach earlier were tourists.

"The kind of friends you hang out with because you have no one else to hang out with."

"Oh, no," I say, surprised. "Those two aren't . . . I mean, I like Celia and Paige."

"Yeah, you like them well enough, I'm sure," Abram says. "But they're not your best friends."

"Yes, they are."

"No, they're not."

"Yes, they are."

"No, they're not." He shakes his head and takes a sip of his water. "You might call them your best friends, you might even *think* they're your best friends, but trust me, they're not."

"How can you say that? You just met me today, and you only talked to them for two minutes."

"I'm a very perceptive person." He shrugs, like this totally explains it.

"Oh, okay," I say, rolling my eyes at his arrogance. "But you're wrong."

"I'm not wrong," he says. He looks at me across the table. "Anyway, why do you care so much if I say they're not your best friends?"

"Because it's a lie," I say. "And it implies that I would be friends with people I don't like. And that's not a very nice thing to say."

"Ah, you weren't listening," Abram says. "I didn't say you didn't like them. I said they weren't your best friends."

I think about why his saying that is making me so defensive. Especially since I've had that same thought myself—the thought that maybe Celia and Paige aren't my best friends, that if they were, I would have told them I didn't get into Stanford. That if they *were* my best friends, they would have listened and consoled me and told me it was going to be okay and reminded me that I'd gotten into Yale, which is a pretty freakin' amazing school, and then we would have gone and planned what I was going to wear on my first day as a Yalie. I wouldn't have had to worry about whether they were going to talk about me behind my back, whether they were secretly happy that I didn't get into Stanford, because it made them feel better about themselves.

*You wouldn't have had to worry about that with Aven and Lyla.*

"I didn't get into Stanford," I blurt.

"What?" Abram looks a little taken aback.

The waitress returns with our meals then, and so I have a second to gather my thoughts before I have to reply.

"Sorry," I say once she's gone. "I just ... I've always wanted to go to Stanford. But I didn't get in. I just found out today." I'm not sure why I'm telling him. It's a crazy thing to just blurt out like that. But suddenly I felt like I needed to say it out loud, like saying it out loud is the first step in admitting it actually happened.

"I'm really sorry," Abram says. "That sucks."

"No, I'm sorry," I say, embarrassed. "I didn't mean to be so random."

"You don't need to apologize," Abram says. "Obviously it's important to you if you wanted to talk about it." He cuts his salmon in half and puts one half on my plate, then reaches over, cuts my hamburger in half, and puts it on his plate. He looks up at me, raising his eyebrows to ask me if the sharing of food is all right with me. "Okay?"

I nod. "Okay." I take a deep breath and tell myself to stop talking about Stanford. He's being nice about it right now, but if I keep babbling, I'm going to seem insane. But I can't help myself. "It's just that when you said that thing about how those girls weren't really my friends—I haven't told them I didn't get into Stanford."

"Because they're not really your best friends."

"I guess not."

"See?" He grins. "I told you I was perceptive."

"It feels stupid, anyway, getting all worked up about not getting into a college. Because in the grand scheme of things I know it doesn't even really matter."

"It matters to you."

"Yeah, but . . ." I trail off, suddenly uncomfortable. I'm going on and on about how I didn't get into Stanford, which probably makes me sound ridiculously stuck up and snobby, not to mention a total bore. I'm supposed to be a mysterious, sexy tourist, not a snotty high school girl who complains about shallow things like her dumb Ivy League rejections.

"Yeah, but what?"

"That's not what we should spend our time talking about."

"It isn't?"

"No."

"Why not?"

"Because it's boring."

"You think because I work at a club that I don't care about things like college acceptances?" He sounds slightly offended.

"No!" I say quickly. "That's not what I meant at all!" And honestly, I didn't. I mean, I didn't think he'd be all that sympathetic about the fact that I didn't get into Stanford. But honestly, who would?

"Sure."

"No, I'm serious, I didn't—"

And that's when I realize he's trying to stop himself from smiling. "Oh," I say. "You're messing with me."

"Of course I'm messing with you!" he says. Then he catches sight of the look on my face. "You okay? Sorry, it seems like maybe that hit close to home."

"No, it's fine. I just don't want you to think I'm a snob."

"I don't think you're a snob."

"You don't?"

He shakes his head slowly. "I think you might be a little guarded, but I don't think you're a snob."

"Guarded?"

"Yeah. Like you might have a hard time letting people in."

I swallow. He's right, and I wonder how he can tell that

about me already. Does he think I'm frigid and closed off? He's not saying it that way, though—he's saying it more like he thinks I'm a puzzle he wants to solve, like if he can just keep moving the pieces around until they finally fit together, he might find something amazing.

"I ordered a cheeseburger in front of you," I say, pushing my now-empty plate toward the middle of the table. "Doesn't that count for not being guarded?"

But before he can answer, the waitress comes back and sets our check down on the table. Abram reaches into his wallet and pulls out his credit card. I go to reach for my purse so I can pay my half, but he stops me. "No way," he says. "I got it."

"Why?"

"Because that's what you do when you take a girl out."

"Oh." I swallow and twist my hands in my lap. "Well, thank you." Is this a date? I'm not sure if meeting a guy in a club and then having him take you out to eat can be considered a date. Don't dates have to be planned in advance, set up, dressed for, etc.? Or is that just me falling back into my old pattern of thinking every single thing has to be planned out? Why can't a date just be meeting someone and doing something spur-of-the-moment? Why can't I stop obsessing about every single little thing?

A warm breeze floats through the air, and an electricity passes between me and Abram. It's like nothing I've ever felt

before. I'm smart enough to know it isn't real—it's just hormones and lust and the headiness of being on vacation and
being with someone I don't know that well.

I think about asking him some questions about
himself—what he does when he's not working at the club, if
he's going to school, if he has any brothers and sisters, what
his favorite color is . . . All the normal things I'd ask someone
I just met. But why? All I know is that I like him. He seems
nice and funny, and does it really matter where he's going to
college or what he's going to do with his future?

*To your parents it does.*

Yeah, but my parents aren't here. And I'm not talking
about marrying this guy. I'm talking about hanging out
with him for one night.

After Abram pays the bill, he looks at me. "So what now,
Cinderella?"

"Cinderella?"

"Yeah. You know, because she had to be home at midnight?"

"Is it midnight already?"

He laughs. "No. I'm asking you if you have to go back to
your hotel now, or if you want to do something else."

*Before graduation, I promise to . . . do something crazy.*

"I want to do something else," I say, before realizing that
maybe I should have tried to play a little hard to get, that I
should have maybe pretended to at least consider wanting to

hang out more instead of just automatically agreeing to it.

"Okay." He tilts his head. "What do you want to do?"

"I don't know," I say. "What do you want to do?"

"We could go for a walk on the beach, or we could go back to the club."

I stay quiet. Neither of those things sounds good to me. The beach is nice, of course, but I don't feel much like walking. And the club is loud and noisy, and Celia and Paige might be back there, getting all up in my business again.

"I'm sick of the beach," I say. "And the club is too noisy."

"Okay." His gaze meets mine across the table, and he's looking at me expectantly, waiting for me to suggest something else. But I don't. I want him to be the one to say it. "Do you want to go back to my house? My parents aren't around." He doesn't elaborate on where his parents are, and I don't ask. As soon as he says the words, I realize how much I want to go with him. I know it's not the smartest thing to do—but he did send Celia a picture of his license, and he did give her his number.

"Sure," I say, trying to sound nonchalant, like going back to his house with him isn't a big deal, even though it's like the biggest deal ever.

"Let's go. My car's back at the club."

He takes my hand as we walk down the street, and his fingers wrapping around mine send a thrill through my body. He leads me behind the Ocean Club to the parking lot. There are a bunch of kids hanging out back there, passing a cigarette back and forth, and I recognize some of them from school.

Abram unlocks his car—it's black and sits high off the ground. He opens the passenger-side door for me, and I see a couple of kids from school watching us. A shiver of excitement flies up my spine. Those kids probably don't know who I am, and even if they did, it's not like they would care what I'm doing. But still. Something about them seeing me makes it feel more real. More exciting.

I settle back into the seat. Abram's car is surprisingly clean. I figured a guy with a job like club promoter who lives on an island probably doesn't care too much about keeping his car clean. But it's actually spotless. It smells like leather and strawberry air freshener.

Abram starts the engine and turns to look at me. "You okay?"

"Yeah," I say. "Let's go."

# NINE

HIS HOUSE ISN'T THAT FAR, AND IT'S ON A nice street, with signs all over that say NEIGHBORHOOD WATCH COMMUNITY and DEED RESTRICTED NEIGHBORHOOD. The houses aren't that big or modern—they're all one-story ranches, like little multicolored boxes lining both sides of the street. It's quiet at this time of night, but streetlights cast a warm glow over everything, and there are lights on in a bunch of different houses, making everything feel warm and inviting.

When we pull into the driveway, I have a moment of panic. Am I really going to do this? But if Abram senses my hesitation, he doesn't show it. Instead, he just gets out and opens my door for me.

"Thanks," I say.

He leads me up the driveway, through the front door, and into the living room. It's tastefully furnished, with dark-brown leather couches, a huge flat-screen television, and a wicker chair in the corner. The floor is dark bamboo with large slats, and there are little straw rugs scattered in every corner. It's cozy and beachy at the same time, and something about the vibe of the house instantly puts me at ease.

Abram throws his keys onto a table by the door and then kicks off his shoes. "Do you want something to drink?" he asks.

I'm not sure if he means alcohol or not, but I say yes, mostly because I want to have something to do.

I follow him to the kitchen, and he opens the fridge and peers inside. "Lemonade, bottled water, soda . . ."

"I'll have a bottled water," I say, figuring it's a safe bet. If he wants to roofie me or something, he won't be able to do it with a sealed bottle of water.

He hands me the drink, and our fingers brush against each other. His hands are warm and soft, and I shiver.

"Thanks." I uncap the water and take a sip.

"You're welcome," he says.

He takes a step closer to me, then takes the bottle out of my hands and drinks. It's a very intimate thing to do—to just drink from my water bottle without asking me first. His eyes lock on mine as he hands it back to me.

The light in the kitchen is one of those dim ones that only lights the countertops, and so it's kind of dark in a sexy, mood-lighting kind of way. I wonder if he hasn't turned on any other lights on purpose, if he's trying to set a tone.

"So," Abram says.

"So."

He takes another step toward me. He's so close now I can see the strong line of his jaw, the tiny little bit of stubble on his chin, the way the collar of his shirt rests perfectly against the curve of his neck. "What should we do now?" he asks softly.

"I don't know." Butterflies are swarming around in my stomach, so hard and so fast I'm afraid they're going to come bursting through my skin. Goose bumps break out on my arms.

"You wanna watch a movie?" he asks. His arms encircle my waist, and he pulls me toward him. His chest is broad and hard, and he smells like a mixture of ocean air, sand, and suntan lotion.

I think about it. Do I want to watch a movie? It's probably the right thing to do. Even if we're going to hook up, shouldn't we at least do something else first? It's just how it's supposed to work—you don't end up back at some guy's house and then immediately jump into bed with him. You have to make him work for it a little bit.

But if I'm being honest with myself, I don't *want* to watch a movie. Sitting on the couch with Abram right next to me, having to pretend to be interested in whatever lame thing is on TV sounds like torture. An exquisite kind of torture, but still torture.

*You can't just hook up with him! That would be so unlike you, so wrong, so . . . not the kind of thing girls like you do.* But what kind of girl am I? The kind of girl who works hard and goes after her goals? And if I am, why can't that kind of girl also be the kind of girl who hooks up with a guy on vacation?

*Before graduation, I promise to . . . do something crazy.*

"I don't want to watch a movie," I say. My voice sounds unsure, and I don't like that. Something about this situation makes me feel like I should not only be in touch with my feelings but also extremely vocal about what it is I want. So I repeat myself. "I don't want to watch a movie."

His eyes burn a little brighter, and I can tell he doesn't want to watch a movie, either. He pushes my hair off my face, and his fingertips burn my skin. "Are you sure?" he whispers.

"I'm sure." This time, my voice sounds decisive on the first try.

Abram moves his lips toward mine, and I close my eyes, waiting for his kiss. As soon as I feel it, I push my body into his, open my mouth, and let his tongue move against mine. He tastes exactly how I expected—like mint and salt water and vacation.

We kiss for what seems like forever, until finally, he pulls back.

"I'm not . . . I mean, we don't have to . . ." He trails off and looks at me. My heart is beating so fast in my chest I'm afraid he can hear it.

"No, it's . . ." I want to tell him it's okay, that I want to, but even though I've already made the decision, saying it out loud seems like it's going too far. Once I say it, I'm not going to be able to take it back. And before I say it, I need to make sure I really, really, really mean it.

He swallows, and his Adam's apple bobs up and down. The stubble on his chin is so amazingly sexy I have to stop myself from kissing him again.

"Do you want to go to my room?" he whispers. His breath tickles my skin, sending a million different feelings—excitement, anticipation, fear, want—shooting up my spine.

"Yes," I say back.

He takes my hand and leads me there.


Abram's bedroom is nothing like I pictured it. I thought it would be a complete mess, with pictures of hot girls on the walls, or maybe posters of indie bands. But his room is neat and plain. You can tell the carpet has been recently vacuumed, and the bookshelves lining the walls are filled with books. A couple of crumpled-up T-shirts and a pair of jeans litter the floor, and there are a few half-empty water bottles on the nightstand, but other than that, the room is clean.

He leads me to the bed, sits down next to me, and starts kissing me again. We kiss until I'm breathless and then, finally, we fall back onto the covers. His fingers move against my skin, up under the back of my shirt, and my body is on fire.

"You okay?" he whispers.

I nod, not trusting myself to speak.

"Do you want to stop?"

I shake my head.

He kisses me again, then reaches down and pulls my shirt over my head. I'm just in my bra now, and I realize I'm more naked with him than I've ever been with anyone in my life. A guy I just met today. He pulls back and looks at me, and I get lost in his eyes. I don't care if I just met him, I don't care that he might never call me again, I don't care that he lives in Florida and is all wrong for me.

All I care about is that he's here, right now, and being with him feels so good. I know I'm looking for an escape from what's going on in my life, from having to deal with my mom, from having to think about the fact that I'm not going to Stanford. But I don't care. All I know is this feels good and perfect and right, and I don't want it to end. "No," I say, "I don't want to stop."

And so we don't.

\* \* \*

When it's over, he holds me close, and for a few seconds my heart is beating fast, but then it slows down and a complete and total feeling of relaxation flows through me. I can't remember ever feeling this relaxed, like my limbs are wet noodles and my stomach is loose, no knot, nothing. *This is what it feels like to live in the moment.*

Abram gets up and grabs more water from the kitchen, handing one bottle to me and setting the other on his nightstand. Then he crosses the room to his dresser, where he pulls out a folded T-shirt and gives it to me.

"Here," he says. "In case you get cold."

"Thanks." I pull it over my head, not because I'm cold, but because suddenly, I feel exposed. I just did the most intimate thing you could do with someone, and now, suddenly, I'm worried about being naked. But as soon as the T-shirt's on, I feel better. It's worn and soft and hits right above my knees, perfect for sleeping.

Sleeping. Am I sleeping here? Or is that too weird? I just assumed I would, with the way he was holding me, but maybe I've overstepped my bounds. I don't even know him. Are you supposed to spend the night with guys you don't even know? In every movie I've ever seen, you do—people are waking up next to strangers all the time.

Abram slides back under the covers and pulls me toward him.

I settle into the crook of his arm, and he reaches into the

nightstand and pulls out a remote.

"Movie?" he asks.

I nod.

He turns on the TV and starts flipping through the channels.

"Say 'stop' if you see something," he says. He clicks past a *Friends* rerun, a true crime show, then gets to a silly Vince Vaughn movie, the one where Vince and Owen Wilson are trying to get internships at Google even though they're both in their forties.

"Stop," Abram and I say at the same time.

I laugh.

"You like this one?" he asks, sounding mildly surprised.

"Yeah," I say. "It's stupid, but in a hilarious way."

"Yeah, and how awesome does it look to work at Google?" he asks.

"Oh, totally. You know I actually googled it to see if it was true?"

"Me too," Abram says.

I prop myself up on my elbow. "You're lying."

"I'm not lying. And besides, someone once told me it's not nice to call someone a liar." His eyes are teasing, and his tone is light. He reaches out and pushes a strand of hair off my face.

"I didn't call you a liar," I say. "I said you were lying."

"Semantics," he says. "And I told you, I'm not lying. They really do have free food at Google."

"And open offices."

"And gorgeous views."

"And nap rooms," I say sleepily.

I lay my head down on Abram's chest, and he plays with my hair, letting the strands fall through his fingers. The rhythm of his touch and the soft hum of the television are soothing, and after a few minutes, my eyelids start to feel heavy. You'd think I'd be too keyed up after the events of the day and what just happened to fall asleep, but it's actually the opposite. I fall right into a deep, dreamless sleep, one of the best rests I've had in a long, long time.

I don't wake until someone starts knocking on the front door at around nine the next morning.

Well, pounding actually.

And ringing the doorbell a few times.

I sit up and blink sleepily. Abram is awake next to me, and he slides his feet out from under the covers and onto the floor. The muscles in his back ripple, and I shiver. I want to do what we did last night all over again.

"Hey," he says, smiling when he sees me. "I'll be right back, okay?"

I nod.

He stands up and disappears down the hallway, back

toward the front door. I take a deep breath and turn away from the sunlight that's filtering in through the blinds. I can hear low voices coming from the doorway. Probably someone selling something. I hope Abram gets rid of them quickly. My eyes are starting to feel drowsy again, and I want to go back to sleep.

But then I hear something that makes me sit up.

Abram's voice, yelling. "You're Quinn's friend?" he's saying.

What? Quinn's friend? What is he talking about? Oh god. Celia and Paige! They must have shown up here, making a big stink about taking me home. Talk about embarrassing! I pop out of bed quickly, before realizing I'm not wearing any bottoms. How can I go outside without any bottoms? I think about putting my clothes from last night back on, but something about wearing a short skirt and tank top outside at this time of day seems . . . wrong.

I creep over to Abram's dresser and pull out a pair of sweatpants, then pull them on. I pause for a second, wondering if he'll think I'm a psycho stalker for just helping myself to his clothes, and then I realize I don't care, because he's going to think I'm even crazier if Paige and Celia start yelling at him.

There's an unfamiliar male voice coming from the doorway, and my heart leaps into my throat as I start hurrying down the hall. Mr. Beals! Could Celia and Paige have told Mr. Beals I wasn't in my room? They said they were going to do room checks! Oh my god! They must have found out I wasn't in my room, and now they're all looking for me. They've probably called my parents; they're probably on their way down here! Why didn't Paige and Celia just text me, why didn't they—

Oh.

It's not Mr. Beals at all.

It's Beckett Cross.

Beckett Cross is standing at Abram's front door. Why would Beckett be at Abram's house? I hardly know him. Unless he's friends with Abram. But Abram never mentioned being friends with someone from my school. And if they're friends, why weren't they hanging out? As I get closer to the front door, Abram turns around.

"Do you know this guy?" he asks me.

"Yeah, I . . . I mean, kind of."

I step out onto the porch so I can talk to Beckett and try to figure out what the hell is going on. And then I see her. Lyla. She's standing on the sidewalk in front of Abram's house, looking around nervously.

"Lyla?" I ask, shading my eyes from the sun to make sure what I'm seeing is right.

"Oh, hi," she says, like it's not a big deal for her to be

showing up at the house of the guy I just slept with. With Beckett Cross nonetheless. Are those two, like, a thing now? I remember how I saw him carrying her bag onto the plane yesterday. Is Lyla still with Derrick? And if she's not, is she with Beckett now? Is she having some kind of breakdown?

"What are you *doing* here?" I demand.

"Just, um . . ." Lyla looks around, like she's trying to figure it out herself. But there's nothing around to explain her presence. In fact, the neighborhood is pretty quiet, except for the chirp of the birds and the sound of the neighbor lady, who's watering her plants with a hose and watching us intently.

"We came to check on you," Beckett says matter-of-factly. He turns and looks to Lyla for confirmation. "Lyla, tell her we came to check on her!"

"Check on her for what?" Abram asks. His tone sounds kind of menacing, like he can't believe anyone would insinuate that he's doing something untoward with me. Even though we did something untoward last night. Can Lyla tell I've been up to no good? I know it's screwed up, but I kind of hope she can. I want her to feel shocked by me, to realize she doesn't know me anymore, that she doesn't know what I'm like or how I behave. *Maybe then she'll realize you've changed and give you another chance.*

"To make sure she was okay!" Beckett says to Abram. He turns to me. "Quinn, are you okay?"

"Yes," I say. "I'm fine!"

"You seem upset," Lyla calls from the sidewalk. "We should probably go."

Oh, for the love of god. Now she's worried about me being upset? She didn't stop to think about that before she showed up here? Am I even upset? I can't decide. On one hand, it's annoying that she's showing up here with Beckett Cross, who I don't even know. On the other hand, it's the first time in two and a half years Lyla's shown any indication that she gives a crap about me, which is actually kind of nice.

"She's fine," Abram says. "Now you want to tell me who the hell you are and what the hell you're doing here?"

"Jesus," Beckett says. "Take a chill pill. We're friends of Quinn's. We just came to make sure she was okay. Which we already told you."

"Quinn, are these people friends of yours?" Abram asks.

I think about it. Beckett definitely isn't my friend, but Lyla . . . I look down to where she's standing at the bottom of the driveway. She's got her arms wrapped around herself and she's moving nervously back and forth, shifting her weight from foot to foot. *Is* she my friend? I want to say yes. But why does she think she has the right to just show up here like this? To just show up here and act like she's all concerned about me, when, let's face it, she's done nothing but blow me off for years. It's not fair. It's not right. My heart softens a little when I think about how she must have been worried enough to come and try to find me. But what made her think it was okay to try to interfere with my life when she knows I want nothing to do with her? It's really incredibly arrogant when you think about it.

"No," I say firmly.

The woman across the street drops her hose onto the ground.

"Bill!" she yells. "Bill, come quick! There's going to be a domestic disturbance."

A domestic disturbance? What is she talking about? She's obviously been watching too many crime shows. This situation is nowhere close to becoming a domestic disturbance.

"No, there's not!" Lyla yells at the woman. "Beckett! Come on! She's fine! Let's go!"

Wow. For someone who's supposedly so concerned, she's giving up pretty quickly. What if I wasn't fine? What if Abram was holding me here against my will, and I had to say I was okay, even though I wasn't, because I was scared of him? Hasn't Lyla ever heard about victims becoming brainwashed by their captors? Elizabeth Smart, hello? And yeah, I'm pretty sure it takes longer than just a day to become brainwashed, but still.

Beckett shakes his head at us one more time, like Abram and I should be happy he and Lyla came out here to check on me, like showing up randomly at someone's house is a good thing instead of something you shouldn't do unless you have a really good reason to think something bad is happening.

Beckett turns around and starts walking down the driveway, and I breathe a sigh of relief. The last thing I wanted was to end up getting into some kind of drama with Lyla and Beckett. One, because I don't even know Beckett, and two, because I don't want to talk to Lyla, and even if I did, the last place I would want to do it is in the driveway of the guy I just lost my virginity to.

My relief is short-lived, though, because as Beckett's walking away, he says, "That guy's an asshole." He's saying it to Lyla, but he says it loud enough so that Abram and I can hear. Actually, I'm pretty sure he *purposely* says it loud enough so Abram and I can hear.

"Hey," Abram calls after him. "What'd you call me?"

Beckett turns around. "I called you an asshole."

Oh, for the love of god.

I look at Lyla, one of those looks like, *Are you seriously going to let this happen right now?* but she obviously doesn't get it, because she just gives me a friendly smile. I scowl and look away. Why is she even here? It's obvious she just woke up, because she's wearing her—

Wait a minute.

Is she wearing my shorts?

"Are those my shorts?" I ask incredulously.

"No," she says. "They're mine." She's lying. I mean, what are the chances that she and I have the exact same shorts? Yes, they're just plain black ones, but still. I thought I'd have to worry about Aven taking my stuff, and now it turns out I have to worry about Lyla, too. No wonder I'm not friends with the two of them anymore. They're a couple of thieves.

"What did you call me?" Abram asks again. He takes a step off the porch and onto the driveway.

"I. Called. You. An. Asshole." Beckett turns around and takes a step closer to the house.

"Come on," Lyla pleads with him, "this isn't any of our business."

Oh, now she's all nervous about people's privacy. Maybe she should have thought about that before she stalked me down wearing my own shorts.

"Get out of here," Abram says.

But Beckett takes another step toward him, and a shot of adrenaline pulses through my body. They're not really going to fight, are they? Over what? Beckett calling Abram an asshole? That seems like a really stupid reason to get into a fight. Is Abram a loose cannon? Is he the type of guy who goes off on someone for no reason? I realize how truly little

I know about him, and it's kind of unsettling.

"Beckett," Lyla says. "Stop. Just stop." There's a certain familiarity in her tone, and I wonder again what the deal is with the two of them. Are they together? They seem like an unlikely match, although like I said, I don't really know that much about Beckett. I'm interested in spite of myself.

From a few streets away comes the sound of a police siren.

"That's the police!" the woman from across the street yells. "My husband has called the police. And as soon as they get here, I'm going to fill out a report. I'm going to fill out a report and make sure that this neighborhood doesn't go the way of the ghetto."

I almost laugh out loud, because she's really getting riled up. And over what? Teenage boys posturing? I'm relieved to realize that if Beckett and Abram really wanted to fight, they would have started by now. I've seen enough stupid fights in the halls at school to realize they start quickly. Yes, there might be a little bit of trash talking, but if people want to fight, they fight.

"Beckett," Lyla says, "please, come on." She sounds freaked out, like she's really worried that the police are going to come and get her in trouble. Well, that's what she gets for crashing my party and trespassing. Then Lyla decides to take it to the next level. "The police are going to come and arrest you!" she screams at Beckett. "Do you want to spend the day in jail?"

She's acting completely ridiculous, and I kind of feel bad for just standing here and watching the whole thing play out. Obviously I would never let Lyla and Beckett go to *jail* just because they wanted to make sure I was okay. Even though it would kind of serve them right.

"Fine," Beckett says to Lyla, "come on." He starts walking backward down the driveway, glaring at Abram the whole time. Abram just stands there, staring him down. Boys! I mean, seriously.

Finally, Beckett and Lyla disappear around the corner.

Abram turns around.

"You okay?" he asks.

"Yeah," I say. "I'm fine." The sun is beating down on us, and I notice for the first time that Abram's not wearing a shirt. It's kind of weird, seeing him out here half-naked. Don't get me wrong, he looks amazing—defined chest, chiseled abs, a flat stomach. . . . But it's one thing to be naked with someone in their bed, it's another to be out here, in the light of day, with someone who doesn't have a shirt on. Also, I'm wearing his clothes.

"I, um, grabbed a pair of sweatpants," I say. "I hope you don't mind."

He grins. "I don't mind."

"Okay."

We just stand there for a moment, and I'm not sure what I'm supposed to do now. Go back to the hotel? Tell him thanks? Give him my number so it doesn't seem like I'm the kind of girl who sleeps with a guy and just expects not to hear from him again? Even though I totally don't expect to hear from him again. Do I? I mean, it wasn't my intention to put any expectations on this when I had sex with him, but now I don't know if—

A police car pulls up across the street. The woman with the hose goes running over to the cops, gesturing at us and pointing excitedly.

Abram sighs. "Sorry," he says. "I'd handle this myself, but they're probably going to want to talk to you, too."

He sounds kind of weary, like he's been through this before and knows exactly what the cops are going to ask and who they're going to want to talk to. I have that same strange feeling again—that I don't really know him, that he could have a criminal record a mile long, or even a warrant out for his arrest.

Suddenly, what seemed exciting and fun last night now just seems ridiculously stupid. Yeah, I didn't get into Stanford, but did I really have to go and jeopardize *every-thing*? I'm sure Yale and Georgetown aren't going to be too thrilled if they find out I've had a run-in with the police. And I think they check that stuff one last time even after you've gotten accepted.

Abram runs back into the house to grab a T-shirt, and when he comes back out, he starts walking down the driveway toward the police car.

And after a second, I take a deep breath and follow him.

# TEN

THE POLICE ARE ACTUALLY REALLY COOL about the whole thing. Since Beckett and Lyla are already gone, there's no one to question except for us. It also helps that the woman across the street (whose name turns out to be Barbara) is a drama queen. Apparently she calls the police, like, a lot. So when the cop shows up, he's a little suspicious of her already.

He asks me if I'm okay, makes a note of the incident, and then drives off. Barbara's pretty disappointed, and she heads into the house, mumbling about how she's going to be writing a letter to her congressman about the police force being completely ineffective.

"That was insane," Abram says once we're back inside.

I follow him to the kitchen, where he pulls out a couple of glasses and fills them with water from the tap.

"I've never been questioned by the police before." I take

the glass from him and take a sip. The water is cool and refreshing.

Abram laughs. "You've never been questioned by the police before?"

I shake my head. "Why is that funny? Are you used to being with girls who have?"

"No, it's just . . . I would hardly call that being questioned by the police."

"We totally were! There was a policeman, and he asked us questions."

This makes him laugh even harder. "Being questioned by the police means they bring you down to the station, sit you in a room, and interrogate you for hours. Talking to a cop in your driveway because some crazy lady across the street freaked out is not being questioned by the police."

"Oh." I take another sip of my water and think about it. "So have you ever been?"

"What? Questioned by the police?"

"Yeah."

He shrugs. "A few times. But nothing they could get to stick. My parents have really good lawyers."

"Oh." A lump comes up into my throat. He's a criminal. I have slept with a criminal.

"I'm just kidding, Quinn," he says, grinning. "You should see your face. No, I've never been questioned by the police." He shakes his head. "What kind of guy do you think I am?"

"Oh, I don't . . . I mean, I don't think you're any kind of guy, really." But I'm kind of shocked to realize I want to find out. Is it because we slept together? He's so not my type. In fact, that was the whole point of having sex with him in the first place. It was supposed to be a one-off, one of those things I could just forget about and move on from.

Am I having some kind of mental breakdown? I've heard about things like this happening—girls who are smart and competent until they go away to college and then *bam*! They start getting drunk and sleeping with frat boys until finally they flunk out. Am I going to flunk out? Am I on a downward spiral? I haven't even graduated high school yet!

"So what do you want to do now?" Abram asks me.

"Oh, um . . . I'm not . . . I don't know." Suddenly, I'm confused. Half of me wants to run out of here, back to my hotel room, back to the safety of my old life. I'll hang out with Celia and Paige and just forget this whole thing ever happened. It'll be a story I'll tell my daughter someday, one of those "you shouldn't have sex before you're ready" stories. Actually, it won't be that kind of story. It was nice, sleeping with Abram. I never felt like I was doing something I didn't want to do, I never felt disrespected or dirty, and we made sure we were safe. He held me all night and kissed me this morning and now he's giving me water and asking me what I want to do today. It's all very confusing. I'm supposed to be heading back to my hotel in the same clothes I wore yesterday, feeling guilty and regretful and wondering what the hell I just did.

But instead I'm here, realizing I want to spend more time with him. This isn't how it was supposed to go. It was supposed to be a night I could just get caught up in, to forget about everything else that was going on in my life. It was supposed to be an escape.

"Are you hungry?" Abram asks. He leans back against the counter and looks at me. "I know a good breakfast place."

I think about it. I'm starving. My stomach feels empty, but not in a bad way. "Yes," I say honestly. "I'm hungry."

"Well, let's go then."

"I need to go back to my hotel first," I say. I look down at what I'm wearing. "I need to shower and change."

"You can shower and change here." He reaches out and pulls me toward him.

I shake my head. "I don't have any clothes here."

"I can find you some clothes."

"What? Your T-shirts and shorts?"

He shrugs. "Yeah. Or you can borrow some of my sister's stuff. She's away at school, she won't mind."

"I don't know . . . ," I say. He's stroking my back now,

his fingers slipping up under the bottom of the T-shirt I'm wearing. His touch feels good on my bare skin, and I shiver. I want to stay here with him, I want to shower here and wear his clothes and just . . . be with him. But I'm scared. How can I not go back to the hotel? I need to talk to Celia and Paige, I need to wear my own clothes, I need to shower and . . . I need to think about everything that happened yesterday. I need to regroup.

"Come on," Abram says, then kisses me softly. "Don't you want to hang out with me?" He puffs out his bottom lip, like he's actually really upset at the thought of me not wanting to spend time with him. I know it's an act. How upset could he be about me leaving when he just met me yesterday? I think about yesterday, seeing him on the beach, talking to those girls in bikinis, the way they were looking at him. If I left, he could probably just head back out to the strip and find another girl to go to breakfast with. Does he do this all the time? Am I just one in a string of dozens of tourists he's brought back to his house and dressed in his clothes and taken out to breakfast?

"Come onnnn," Abram says. "You have to eat." He takes my hand and starts pulling me down the hall toward his bedroom. He stops at a linen closet and pulls out a towel and a fresh bottle of shampoo. "Here you go," he says. "Herbal Essences, girls love that."

I want to ask him how he knows what girls like, but something tells me I won't like the answer.

He brings me to his room. "Sit," he commands.

I sit on the bed while he disappears back down the hall. I pick up my phone. Texts from Celia and Paige, demanding to know where I am, threatening to call the police if I don't answer. Which is pretty dramatic. Also they couldn't have been that worried, because even though they threatened to do something, obviously they did nothing. They didn't try to find me, they didn't call the police, they didn't try to figure out where I was or what I was doing. (Although I guess it was pretty obvious.) In fact, the only one who seemed to really give a crap about me was Lyla. I text Celia and Paige back and tell them I'm fine, even though they don't deserve it.

Abram reappears in the doorway, holding a pair of gray yoga pants, a purple tank top, and a pair of flip-flops.

"My sister's," he says, proud of himself. "They still have the tags on and everything."

"Thanks." I take the stuff, but I don't move from the bed. Is this really how I want to spend my senior trip? Hanging out with a random guy I just met? Shouldn't I be on the beach, hanging with Celia and Paige, experiencing my last moments with them and my classmates before we all graduate and go our separate ways?

My phone vibrates.

My mom.

Calling me.

To talk about Stanford, to talk about how I didn't get in, to talk about how disappointing the whole thing is. She loves that word. *Disappointing.* She won't come out and say *I'm* a disappointment, but she has no problem letting me know *situations* are disappointing, or that I've let her down in some way.

I don't feel like dealing with that right now. I don't feel like dealing with Celia and Paige, either. Just because they're in my class and just because this is our senior trip doesn't mean I have to spend it with them, doing things I don't want to do. I should be doing what I *want*, what sounds fun to me, what makes me happy.

And right now, what I want is to spend time with Abram.

So I send my mom's call to voice mail.

"Okay," I say, smiling. "Let's go to breakfast."

"Are you carbs or protein?" Abram asks as we walk down Ocean Boulevard an hour later.

"Carbs or protein?"

"Yeah, you know . . . like are you a waffles and pancakes kind of girl, or do you stick with your standard eggs and bacon?"

"Oh." I think about it. I don't go out to breakfast that often—weekend mornings are for studying or working on school projects and applications—but when I do, I always get the same thing. Western omelet, wheat toast, and home fries. But now that order seems completely boring. Of all the things I could get, I pick *wheat toast*? What about Belgian waffles or crepes or even eggs Benedict? Why do I have to be a wheat toast and omelet kind of girl? Do I even like wheat toast and omelets? Suddenly I'm not so sure. Suddenly I'm the kind of girl who hooks up with random boys. And the kind of girl who hooks up with random boys doesn't eat something as boring as plain old wheat toast.

"Pancakes," I say. "Definitely. Chocolate chip ones. With a side of bacon."

Abram grins, like he approves of this choice. "I should have known," he says. "Any girl cool enough to order a barbe-cue bacon cheeseburger isn't going to settle for an omelet."

I flush. I like the fact that he called me cool, that he thinks I'm the kind of girl who does cool things.

We continue walking down the main street of Siesta Key, along with the tourists in their beachwear. Everyone else is heading toward the water, while we're going in the opposite direction, toward the restaurants. Of course, this means we have to dodge people as we weave in and out of the crowds, but it's kind of okay because otherwise I'd have to talk to Abram, and I'm not sure exactly what to say.

It feels weird making conversation with someone you've

already slept with. What am I supposed to ask him? All the stupid small-talk stuff that you ask when you're on a first date with someone? That seems so weird, since he's actually . . . seen me naked.

Oh my god, he's seen me naked. I have a flash of him last night, on top of me, the moonlight shining through the window, his arms wrapped around me, his lips on mine. I flush hot. Oh my god.

I. Had. Sex. With. Him.

What the hell was I thinking? What seemed daring and crazy last night now just seems ridiculously reckless. I'm completely different than I was yesterday. I'm not a virgin anymore. Abram will forever be in my memories, will forever have the place of being the first person I had sex with. I suddenly feel very world-weary and grown-up. Does everyone walking down the street know we slept together? I know that's ridiculous. People can't tell just by looking at you if you've had sex or not.

But still. If they knew, they wouldn't be surprised. A guy and a girl, out in comfy-looking clothes late in the morning, their hair disheveled. Not that my hair is that disheveled. I made sure I brushed it this morning after my shower, using the brush I always keep in my purse. It's not good to brush your hair when it's wet, but I didn't want to make it too obvious that I'd been up to something nefarious.

This whole sleeping-with-someone thing is very confusing. It is a BIG DEAL. And here I am, just going out to breakfast like it's nothing, like everything's the same. How can I think of food at a time like this?

I should be . . . I don't know, doing whatever it is people do after they have sex for the first time. I should be telling Celia and Paige about it, I should be dissecting it moment by moment, I should be calling my mom to share the news. My mom! Ha! The whole Stanford thing aside, my mom and I don't have the kind of relationship where we share things like that.

Even if everything was fine and I'd gotten my acceptance letter the way I wanted, I wouldn't have called her to tell her I'd lost my virginity. The only things we bond over are things like grades and academics and working hard. The only time I ever tried to bond with my mom over something else, the only time I went to her for advice, it was a disaster. So much of a disaster it ended up costing me my friendship with Lyla and Aven.

"So here's the thing," Abram's saying now, and I realize I was so caught up in my thoughts I didn't even realize we're standing outside a cute little breakfast place. Tables spill out onto a huge outdoor patio, and umbrellas are set up all over, blocking patrons from the sun. Every table is full, and there are a couple dozen people hanging out on the stone benches outside, waiting for tables. "This place has the best breakfast on the key. Which is obvious, because there's a wait." He leans in close to me and whispers in my ear. "Although most of these people are tourists, and they're just here because they saw the place and so they stopped because it's convenient. They're lucky, because the breakfast is amazing, but they're also annoying because they're taking up our spot."

He's so close that his breath tickles my ear, and I can see the tiny bit of stubble that's starting on his jaw. My breath catches in my chest. How is it possible to be this attracted to someone I don't even know?

"Oh," I say dumbly.

"So," Abram says. "We can wait for a table, or we can get our breakfast to go."

"Get it to go?" My voice sounds weak. Does he mean get it to go and then take it back to his house with us? If we go back to his house, I'm definitely going to sleep with him again. I can already feel how badly I want to.

"Yeah. I know a great place we can eat. Near the beach."

Oh. He doesn't mean go back to his house. I don't know if I'm disappointed or relieved.

"Okay," I say. "Sounds good."

Twenty minutes later, we're joining the crowd of people on their way down to the beach, bags of food in our hands. Well, actually not in our hands. In Abram's hands. He insisted on carrying my bag for me.

"So have you been to Florida before?" he asks as we walk.

"Um, just once when I was really little. My grandparents took me and my brother to Disney World."

"Did you have fun?"

"All I remember is throwing up on the teacup ride and then crying."

Abram laughs. "So, no then." He turns and looks at me. "Well, hopefully this time your trip will be a little more memorable."

*It already is,* I want to say. But I don't. I can't. I don't know if he knew I was a virgin, and I'm not going to tell him. I don't want to freak him out, make him think that I'm going to become all psycho obsessed with him or something.

We walk all the way down the main road, past the main part of the beach, until we're almost at the very end of the street. There are beach access points all off the main road, and we end up at the very last one, following the path until we hit the rocky part of the sand.

"This is going to be tricky," Abram says, looking over his shoulder at me. "Do you have good balance?"

"What do you mean by good?" I ask warily. My balance is not the best. I almost got a B in gym because I kept falling off the balance beam during our gymnastics unit. I had to do a whole bunch of extra credit so I could get my grade up. (I couldn't end up with a B in anything, because that would have brought my whole grade point average down, and if I wanted to get into Stanford, I needed it to be perfect. Looking back, I should have just let myself fall off the damn beam and not worried about it.)

Abram laughs. "Just pay attention, you'll be fine." Obviously he never saw me in Ms. Mercurio's fifth-period coed gym class.

I take a breath and keep walking. At the very end of the beach, right before the sand curves around and disappears out of sight, there are a bunch of vacation houses with stone walls in front of them. Abram jumps up onto one and disappears around the bend.

I stand there, hesitating, until he pops his head back around and looks at me.

"You coming?"

"I don't know." I glance at the wall. I can't see what's around the corner. "Isn't it . . . I mean, isn't it trespassing?"

He cocks his head and thinks about it. "I guess. But only for a second. Think of it not like trespassing but more like cutting through someone's yard."

"I guess that's not so bad." But I still stay frozen in place. I don't like breaking rules. *You already broke a pretty big one; walking on someone's stone wall in the middle of the day is not the end of the world.*

Abram holds his hand out, and I reach up and grab it.

He pulls me up beside him in such an unexpectedly fluid motion that I almost lose my balance.

"Whoa," he says, steadying me with his hand. "You okay?"

"Yeah." I'm dizzy from his closeness. I drop his hand. "I'm fine." I regain my footing and follow him around the wall. We have to walk single file because it's so narrow, but it gives me a chance to try and slow my heart rate down.

When we get to the end of the wall, Abram jumps off, making it look easy. He's holding our bags and everything, and he doesn't lose his footing on the sand below for even a second. I sit down on the wall, then gingerly push myself off, and even then I have to take a big step forward to keep myself from falling over.

"Nice job," Abram says.

"Sarcastic?"

"No, not at all. I'm impressed you didn't fall or ask for help."

I wonder why he's surprised. Does he bring girls here a lot? Is this just the last step in an oft-repeated performance? Has he let tons of other girls sleep over before taking them out to breakfast while they're wearing his sister's clothes? Maybe he doesn't even have a sister. Maybe she's completely made up, and he just buys the clothes and then puts them in a random room. I *thought* it was kind of suspicious that the clothes fit me so well—he must pick things out in a variety of sizes.

We walk farther and farther down the beach, past different houses and apartment buildings, until we get to a stretch where there's nothing but sand and water. Right when I'm about to ask him where we're going (let's face it, he's pretty much a stranger—what if he's taking me somewhere shady?), the beach narrows and a small inlet appears.

We turn the corner into a rocky cove, and the view is breathtaking. Palm trees cast shade onto the sand, the ocean sparkles in the morning sun, and gulls dance and swoop across the sky.

Abram sits down on one of the huge rocks that line each side of the inlet.

"Worth it?" he asks as I take in the view.

"So worth it." I sit down next to him, then kick my flip-flops off and let my toes dangle into the ocean. The water is warmer than I would have expected.

Abram rustles through the bags and hands me a Styro-foam box. I open it to reveal the most delicious-looking pair of chocolate chip pancakes I've ever seen—plate-sized and covered with a pat of butter that's just about finished melt-ing. A small plastic container of dark maple syrup is nestled in the corner of the box, along with three strips of crispy bacon and a small fruit salad.

"Thanks," I say as Abram opens his own box, showing an identical breakfast.

"Sure."

"You got the same thing as me."

"No, *you* got the same thing as *me*."

I shake my head and take a bite of pancake. It's light, fluffy, and sweet. I close my eyes and take a moment to savor its taste and the feel of the sun warming my skin.

"Good, right?"

"So good."

We sit there for a few seconds, not saying anything, until finally Abram wipes his mouth and looks at me seriously. "So listen," he says. "I think . . . I mean, I need to talk to you about last night."

"Oh. Um, okay." The pancakes immediately turn to stone in my stomach. Why do we have to talk about what happened last night? That definitely can't be good. What can really be said about it, anyway? That it was fun? That it was nice? That he doesn't want me to think it means anything? Because those are things that don't really need to be said.

Oh god. Maybe he's going to tell me something even worse than that. Like that I'm really bad at sex. Am I horrible in bed? How does one even fix that? Can you learn to be good at sex, or is it just a natural talent?

Maybe I'll just have to become a virgin again. Then I can say I'm saving myself for marriage, and whatever guy I end up with won't have to know I don't know what I'm doing until it's too late. Of course, it won't *technically* be true, the whole saving-myself-for-marriage thing, since I've already had sex with Abram, but still. I can become one of those born-again virgins.

I saw a show about that once—these three girls were all, like, forty or something and they lived in a house together and they were all waiting to have sex until they were married. And one of them was a born-again virgin. She'd had sex with a bunch of guys when she was younger, and then she decided not to do that anymore until she got married. Is that what I should do? Have a bunch more sex before I decide to become born-again?

But isn't that kind of . . . dangerous? It sounds like a surefire way to end up with an STD. Oh my god. Does Abram have an STD? We used a condom, but still. Those things aren't one hundred percent.

Abram takes a deep breath and sets his container of pancakes down on the rocks next to him. I immediately take it as a bad sign. Why does he have to set his pancakes down? You only set your food down in the middle of eating it if you have something really serious to say.

"I just want you to know that I don't do that all the time," he says.

"Do what?"

"Take girls back to my house."

I look at him incredulously. "You've never taken a girl back to your house before?" Seriously? Does he really expect me to believe that? There's no way. I saw the way he was on the beach yesterday, handing out those flyers, the way girls were responding to him, looking at him like they wanted to jump on him right there.

"No, I didn't say that." He grins at me, but I look away.

"Look," I say. "If this is the part where you try to make me feel better about sleeping with you, you can save it."

"No!" He shakes his head. "Wow, I'm really screwing this up." He takes another deep breath and then turns and looks at me. "Yes, I have hooked up with girls I've met on the beach before, or in the club. But what happened last night, that was . . . I just want you to know I don't do that all the time." He's looking at me, his eyes serious, like he wants me to know last night meant something to him. Longing fills my body. I want to believe him so badly. But how can I? Of course he's going to say he doesn't do that all the time, if only because he knows it'll make it easier to sleep with me again. I feel like he's expecting me to say something, but I don't know what to say that won't make me sound completely crazy.

"Okay," I say finally. "Well, thanks for telling me that."

"You're welcome," he says, and a brief look of disappointment crosses his face, and then there's a bit of an awkward moment between us, and I wish I could go back and say what happened last night was special to me, too, but before I can, he picks up his pancakes and starts eating.

I do the same. "So you've lived here your whole life?" I ask, in an effort to gloss over the weirdness.

"Yup," he says. "Born and raised. Same house and everything."

"You've lived in the same house your whole life?"

"Yeah."

"Wow. My mom would never allow that. She loves to move."

"Really? So you've gone to a bunch of different schools?"

I shake my head. "No, we always stay in the same town. She likes the school district. But she loves to move all around, looking for the best houses. She's kind of a snob." As soon as the words are out of my mouth, I regret them. Sitting here with a perfect stranger, telling him my mom's a snob, seems like a breach of trust. I've never called my mom a snob before, to anyone. So to call her that to a guy I don't even know seems really unfair.

"Is that why you were so concerned about coming off as snobby last night?"

My heart does a double beat. Coming off as snobby last night? Did he think I was inhibited while we were hooking up? But then I remember telling him at the restaurant that I probably sounded like a snob since I was complaining so much about not getting into Stanford. "Yeah, maybe," I say. I dip my toes farther into the ocean. The sun is rising higher in the sky, and I turn my face toward it, not caring that I'm not wearing any sunscreen, not caring that I might get a little bit of a burn. It feels good, and so I'm going with it. "I shouldn't put it all on my mom, though. I mean, she's set up all these expectations for me, but I'm the one who bought into the whole thing."

"What kind of expectations?"

"Mostly school stuff," I say. "Stanford."

"But you didn't get in."

I shake my head. "No."

"So what will you do?"

I shrug. "Go to Yale, maybe. Or Georgetown."

Abram gapes at me. "You got into Yale and George-town?"

"Yeah." Suddenly, I'm embarrassed. I don't like it when people make a big deal about where I'm going to school or how smart I am. You'd think I'd be used to it by now—it's been happening since I was in kindergarten. But it makes me uncomfortable.

"That's insane," he says. "That's amazing." He shakes his head. "You must be so happy."

"Yeah," I say. "I am." But now I'm embarrassed for another reason—the truth is, I'm *not* happy about Yale or Georgetown. I'm just upset about Stanford. Talk about the glass being half-empty. "Actually," I say, "that's a lie. I'm not happy about it."

"You don't want to go to school at either of those places?"

"I wanted to go to Stanford," I say. "At least, I thought I did." I shake my head. "Now I'm just . . . confused."

"It's okay to be confused," he says simply, like he doesn't care about the fact that I didn't get into the school I wanted, that I'm sitting here next to him complaining about having to choose between two great schools. "But if you didn't get into Stanford, it probably happened for a reason."

"You think?"

"Yeah." He grins. "I think everything happens for a reason." He turns to look at me, his eyes locking on mine. "Like how you were on the beach yesterday at the exact moment I was."

I grin. "Oh, yeah," I say. "And what was the reason that happened?"

He grins back. "So we could be here, right now, together." He kisses me softly on the lips.

"Talking about what a snob I am?"

"I don't think you're a snob at all."

"Thanks," I say. I don't know why, but it means something to hear him say that. He's just so easy to talk to, so nonjudgmental, such a good listener. I can tell he's not the type of person to say something just because he knows you want to hear it—so when he tells me he doesn't think I'm a snob, I believe him.

I'm done with my pancakes and bacon, and all that's left in my container is fruit salad. I fork up a strawberry and eat it.

Abram's food is completely gone, and he takes his fork and sticks it into my fruit salad, spearing a piece of pineapple.

"You really don't care about taking other people's food, do you?" I ask.

He grins and pops the pineapple into his mouth. "Hey, I left you the good stuff," he says. "I took the pineapple. Everyone knows that's the worst part of a fruit salad."

"What if I love pineapple?" I ask. "What if pineapple is my very favorite fruit in the whole entire world and you've just deprived me of it?"

"Oh, I'm sorry," he says, pretending to be apologetic. "I didn't mean to deprive you." He spears another piece of pineapple and holds it out to me, and I lean down and eat it off his fork.

"Yum," I say. "Pineapple. Best fruit ever."

He laughs and shakes his head, then brushes his thumb against my lower lip. His eyes are on mine, and a breeze blows through the palm trees, ruffling the leaves. "Pineapple juice," he explains.

"Thanks," I say softly.

But he doesn't move his thumb away. It stays there, brushing against my lip for a moment, before his whole hand moves to my chin and pulls me toward him. His mouth is on mine, soft and sweet, different than it was last night. Last night our kisses were hungry, like we were both trying to prove something, like we were both trying to lose ourselves in each other or at least in what we were doing.

But today his kiss feels softer, more searching. Kissing

him last night left me breathless and frenzied—kissing him today is more of a slow, steady burn.

After a few minutes, he pulls back and looks at me.

"Hi," he says, smiling.

"Hi."

He leans back on the rock and looks at me. "So what do you want to do today?"

"Today?"

"Yeah. What should we do?"

"I don't know." I wasn't planning on hanging out with him today. I wasn't planning on any of this.

"Are you up for something fun?" he asks.

"Um, duh. Always," I say. It's meant to be sarcastic, but then I realize he doesn't know me that well. All he knows about me is that I had sex with him last night, that I met him on the beach and then went home with him, that I ditched my friends to hang out with him, and that I didn't get into Stanford, which probably means he has no idea that I *should* have gotten into Stanford, that I'm the kind of girl who works hard and plays by the rules and doesn't ever do anything that's even remotely fun.

"Cool," he says. He starts to pack up the remnants of our breakfast, picking up the empty containers and used silverware and putting them in one of the plastic bags. I marvel again at the ease with which he moves, with the easy way he just asked me to spend the day with him. There was no stressing over it, no wondering what I was going to say, no worrying I was going to turn him down or think he was crazy for suggesting it. Is this how normal people live? Or just him?

We walk back through the cove and out onto the beach, and this time, when we go over the tricky part of the wall, he holds my hand tight.

We make a plan to meet back up on the beach in an hour. As nice as it was being able to wear Abram's sister's yoga pants, it's time for me to change into my own stuff. Abram wouldn't tell me where we were going—all he said was to wear a bathing suit and clothes that I wouldn't mind getting wet. So obviously it has something to do with the water. But on a barrier island like Siesta Key, that could mean a million different things.

When I get back to the hotel, no one's in my room. I breathe a sigh of relief. Not that it would have really mattered—I'm only going to be here for a few minutes, just long enough to change. But still. I want to limit my interactions with Lyla and Aven as much as possible.

I brush my hair until it shines, then quickly go over it with the straightening iron, flipping it up at the ends so it falls in beachy waves. It will probably get completely wrecked once I'm in the water, but hopefully it'll last at least until I'm on the beach. I add a quick slick of pink gloss to my lips and a swipe of bronzer to my cheeks. It's a lot different from the smoky eye I was wearing last night, but I'm hoping Abram can appreciate my more casual look.

I'm just about to head back out when my phone buzzes with a text.

Paige.

COME DOWN HERE IMMEDIATELY

Wow. Demanding, much?

I text back, *What?*

Come down to our room.

I hesitate. I don't really *want* to go down to their room. They're going to be asking me tons of questions about last night. Do they know I never came home? Did they come to my room and look for me? Were they really going to call the police? How angry are they that I never texted them?

I wonder if I can get away with pretending I'm not here, that I'm still out at Abram's.

But a second later, my phone buzzes again.

I saw you coming in the lobby, so I know you're here.

Great. Well, there goes that plan, I guess.

Whatever. It's not the end of the world to go down and check in with Celia and Paige. Actually, it will probably be good for them to see that I haven't been chopped up into a million pieces, that I'm totally okay and happy. That way when I tell them I'm going to be spending the day with Abram, they won't give me crap for it.

But when I knock on the door to Celia and Paige's room, they're not in good moods.

"Where the hell have you been?" Paige accuses as soon as she opens the door. Her hair is pulled back in a ponytail, and she obviously just woke up, because she's wearing her glasses.

"Good afternoon to you, too, Paige," I say brightly.

"Do you know how worried we've been about you?" she asks. "We thought you were dead!"

"Why would you think I was dead?" I ask, as she moves aside and lets me walk by her into the room. "You knew I was with Abram."

This seems to throw her a little bit, and she shakes her head. "Yeah, but you never came back last night."

"Why are you giving me such a hard time?" I ask. "You guys ditch me all the time."

Paige's eyes bug out of her head. "We do not!"

"Yes, you do."

"No, we don't."

"Yes, you do." The thing at Bronx's birthday party where Celia left me was just the latest incident. They both abandon me constantly—at parties, at school, on random Saturday nights when one of them decides they want to go home with some guy or hang out with some guy instead of all of us hanging out as a group.

It's annoying that Paige is giving me crap for something the two of them do on a regular basis. But whatever. I'm in too good of a mood for her to bring me down. Plus, I want to get out of here before it starts getting late.

Paige throws her hands up in the air and then shakes her head, like I'm the one who's being ridiculous. "Look, just forget it, okay? You're going to be around today, right? Because I need help."

She turns away, and that's when I see Celia, lying in bed. She's got one of those eye masks over her eyes to block out the sunlight that's streaming through the window, and there's a washcloth on her head. "Stop talking so loud," she grumbles. "Seriously, you guys are, like, screaming. It's too early for that."

"It's not too early," I say, sighing. "You're just too hung-over."

"It's not my fault," she moans. "Those guys last night, they kept buying us drinks." She says it like she was a completely innocent party in the whole thing, like she hadn't specifically gone over to them with the intent of getting them to buy her as many drinks as possible. I saw those guys—they were harmless. They didn't seem like the type to ply innocent girls with alcohol in an effort to get them wasted. They seemed nice, and they probably kept buying drinks because Celia and Paige had somehow convinced them that Celia could hold her liquor.

"You didn't have to drink them," I say. I walk over to the bed and sit down next to her.

She lifts up her eye mask and blinks in the sun. Her eyes are a little watery, but they're not bloodshot or anything, and her pupils and focus seem fine. However bad she feels right now, there's no reason to think there's anything really wrong with her. She probably just needs to sleep it off and get rehydrated, like she did yesterday.

I reach for the bottle of water that's sitting on the nightstand and open it.

"Drink," I command.

Celia takes a tiny sip. "I'm never going to drink again," she says. "I promise." She does the sign of the cross, which makes no sense, since she's not even Catholic. Maybe she means she crosses her heart, but still.

I sigh. "I've heard that one before."

"No, this time I mean it," she says. She looks at me hopefully. "Quinn, will you order me a pizza?"

I glance doubtfully at the trash can that's sitting next to her bed. Obviously it's been put there for a reason.

"I haven't thrown up in two hours," Celia says, catching me looking.

"She hasn't," Paige confirms. She flops onto her bed

and turns on the TV. "So you can definitely order her pizza. Then after she eats it, maybe she'll feel okay enough to go to the beach."

I look at her incredulously as she flips to a *Golden Girls* rerun. On the screen, Sophia is making fat jokes about Blanche's daughter. The jokes are tasteless and mean, but Paige laughs and throws her head back. "I just love this show," she says. She glances at me and Celia. "Promise me we'll be like that when we get old and our husbands are dead?"

"Of course," Celia says. She squints at the screen. "But we'll have a way better house than that. And we'll be better dressed. No old-lady clothes." She leans back on the pillows.

I have a moment of panic thinking about the three of us living together as old women. Is that how my life is going to turn out? Am I going to be living with Paige and Celia, in some little house in Miami, taking care of Celia when she gets drunk and tries to flirt with the pool boy? Am I going to be fixing her meals and trying to hide in my room so she doesn't ask me to order her a pizza? The thought is so horrible I almost want to throw up into the trash can myself.

"Quinn," Celia moans. She pulls her eye mask back down over her eyes. "Can you please order my pizza now? Not from the place we got it yesterday, it was too greasy."

"Yeah, and can we get half with just veggies?" Paige pipes up. "I want to limit my meat consumption. I'm feeling a little bloated."

"Thank you, Quinn, so much," Celia murmurs, patting my arm. "You're saving my life."

I look at them, stunned. Do they really expect me to order them pizza and then sit here, wasting my senior trip in this room watching *Golden Girls* reruns until Celia feels better?

I stand up. "I have plans today," I announce.

Paige turns and looks at me incredulously, and Celia props herself back onto her elbow before sliding her eye mask up again. "What kind of plans?" Celia asks.

"With Abram," I say, liking the way it sounds. *With Abram.* Like having plans with him is natural, like we're a set. Quinn and Abram. Hanging out together. Making plans.

"The guy from last night?" Paige asks. She and Celia exchange a glance.

"Yes, the guy from last night," I say.

"Quinn, honey, are you sure that's a good idea?" Celia asks. "I mean, I know he's cute and all, but where could it really go?"

"It doesn't have to go anywhere," I say. "I'm just having fun."

Paige and Celia exchange another look, like I couldn't

possibly hook up with a guy just for fun.

Is that what they think of me? That I'm so lame that even when I say I'm having fun, there's no way I could possibly *really* be having fun?

"I am perfectly capable of having fun," I tell them.

"Oh, Quinn, honey, of course you are," Celia says. "And I'm glad you had fun last night." She takes a deep breath. "I just really need my friends right now. Both of you. Paige, you'll order the pizza, right? For all of us?"

"Sure," Paige says, suddenly sounding nervous. "What kind do you want, Quinn?" Now that I'm sticking up for myself, she's afraid I really am going to leave. And if that happens, she's going to have to take care of Celia by herself.

"I'm going to meet Abram," I say.

"But I'm sick!" Celia cries. She sounds just as panicked as Paige, and I realize it's for the same reason—with me gone, she's going to be stuck having to rely on Paige to take care of her. And Paige isn't as good at that as I am.

"You're not sick," I tell her. "You're just hungover. You'll feel better as soon as you drink some more water and get some carbs in you." I push the water bottle closer to her so she can drink.

She just stares at me.

Paige just stares at me, too.

"Okay, then," I say. "So I guess I'll see you guys a little later?"

"You're not seriously leaving?" Celia says. She sounds very strong for someone who's supposedly so sick.

"Yes, I am," I say. "I told you, I have plans."

"You're ditching us," she says, "for some local guy with a bad surfer haircut?"

"He doesn't have a bad surfer haircut," I say, wondering why she would even say such a thing. Abram doesn't have a bad haircut. Everything about him is sexy and cool and just . . . I shiver.

"You can't go," Celia says. "You need to stay here and help us. We're friends. Friends don't leave each other for some random guy."

"He's not random," I say.

"He *is* random!" Celia says, pulling off her eye mask and tossing it onto the bed. "You just met him last night, and now suddenly you're taking off with him!"

"Oh, like how you took off with Bronx at his birthday party a few weeks ago?" I shoot back. "And just left me there like an idiot and I had to call my brother to come and pick me up?"

"That was different!" Celia says. "You knew I'd been wanting to hook up with Bronx for months!"

"Oh, okay," I say. "So if we've been wanting to hook up with a guy for a while, then it's okay to just ditch each other?

But if we haven't, then it's not okay? I'm just trying to figure out the rules of our friendship, because you seem to keep changing them."

"Okay, guys," Paige says. She reaches over and clicks off the TV and then moves so she's perched on the edge of the bed, her knees folded underneath her. "That's enough. Let's just take a time-out."

"I don't want to take a time-out," I say.

"You're being really selfish," Celia says, shaking her head. "And someday you're going to realize what you're doing. That you're blowing us off for some random guy you don't even know."

"Stop calling him random!" I practically scream.

"But he is random!" Celia yells.

"I think what Celia means is—," Paige tries, but it's too late. We've started fighting, and we're not going back.

"You just met him last night!" Celia says. "You can't choose some guy you just met over your best friends. You probably won't even remember him in two months. Guys come and go, Quinn, but friendship is forever."

I cross my arms over my chest. "Yes, I will," I say. "I will remember him because we slept together."

Paige gasps.

Celia gasps.

"You did not!" Celia says.

"We did too!" I say, enjoying the shocked look on their

faces. "And so I would really appreciate it if you stopped calling the boy I lost my virginity to a random."

And then I turn and walk out of the room without saying good-bye.

# ELEVEN

I'M ACTUALLY QUITE CALM ABOUT THE WHOLE thing. Like, I don't even care that I'm fighting with Celia and Paige. I don't even care that I just blurted out the fact that I lost my virginity without building up to it or discussing it or telling them how it went. I don't care that they're probably both really mad at me.

In fact, instead of feeling worried or anxious, I feel free. It doesn't matter that Celia's back in her room all hungover and wanting a pizza, because for the first time in a while, it's not my problem. I don't have to deal with her.

All I have to do is walk down this beautiful beach toward this beautiful ocean to where I said I'd meet Abram. I don't have to worry about anything—not Stanford, not my internship, not Celia . . . nothing. Just this moment. The thought is so freeing that it takes everything inside of me to stop myself from twirling around on the sand like some kind of lunatic.

When I get to the place I'm supposed to meet Abram, he's not there yet. So I sit down on the sand and shade my eyes from the sun and take in deep breaths of ocean air, letting the breeze blow a mist of salt water onto my face. But after a couple of minutes, I'm starting to get worried. Is it possible he's not coming? He wouldn't stand me up, would he? My stomach churns, but before I can morph into full-blown panic mode, I see him down the beach, walking toward me. He smiles as soon as our eyes meet, and my heart speeds up.

*I like him. I like him a lot.*

The thought surprises me. That's not the way this was supposed to go. I was supposed to hook up with him and then just forget about him. I can't actually *like* him. That's ridiculous. And silly. He lives in Florida. And I hardly know him.

"Hey!" he says. "I'm so glad you're still here. I was getting worried, thinking you might give up on me."

"Nope," I say dumbly, because now that's he's back in close proximity, I'm remembering just how hot he is. He's wearing a navy-blue T-shirt, and his arms are cut and defined. His green-and-blue board shorts hang low on his hips, and I remember his six-pack and how perfect his chest was, and . . . suddenly, I'm all keyed up.

"Sorry I was late," he says. "I was having trouble finding a parking spot, and then I had to wrestle this off the top of my car." I realize he's been dragging something behind him, and I look to see what he's talking about. It's a box. Or . . . not a box. More like a square-shaped container? It's about four feet by two feet, and it looks kind of heavy.

"What is that?" I ask.

"It's a boat."

"Like, to go out on the water with?" I peer at it closely. "And it's in there? But how does it fit?"

"It's not in there," Abram says, laughing. He kneels down in the sand and motions me to do the same. "This *is* the boat. It's folded up."

I frown. "A folded-up boat? But it's made out of cardboard!"

"It's not made out of cardboard. It's high-quality fiberglass." He knocks on it.

"Fiberglass?" I reach out and touch it. He's right. It is fiberglass. Weird.

"Well, yeah. Fiberglass and a little wood. It's lighter than a regular boat, and it folds up for easy storage." I watch as he unfolds the boat and puts it together, using string ties and folding flaps into each other. The whole process takes only a couple of minutes, and when he's done, sure enough, there's a small canoe-like boat sitting on the sand.

"That is so cool," I say, running my finger along the side of it. "Where did you get this?"

"I made it."

"You *made* it?"

"Yup." He stands up and brushes his hands together until the sand is gone.

"But you're going to be rich!" I say, standing up next to him. "You need to bring this to someone, like a . . . I don't know, a boating company."

He laughs. "I'm still perfecting it. It's way too heavy right now to be practical. One of the things I need to work on is making it more portable. But thanks for the vote of confidence." He pushes the boat down the sand toward the water, until the front part slides into the ocean. A couple of people walking by turn to look at it. It does look a little bit strange, like it shouldn't be floating. But it *is* floating, its nose or whatever it's called (the bow? the stern?) bobbing merrily in the water.

"Come on," Abram says, wading into the water.

I take a deep breath and then follow him. "I'm scared," I say after a few steps. "What if we capsize?"

"Quinn, I'm offended," he says, teasing. "Are you trying to imply that not only would I build a boat that's not seaworthy but that I would dare to take you out on it?"

I look into the boat. "How do you drive it?" I ask.

He laughs again. "You don't drive it, you paddle it."

"Oh. Um, are you going to be paddling it?"

"Me and you," he says. "Both of us."

"Oh." I have a vision of me holding a paddle and then

dropping it in the water right before the whole boat turns over and we end up lost at sea. For years.

"Don't worry," Abram says, like he's reading my mind. "You'll be fine."

"That sounds like something someone says at the beginning of a horror movie," I say. "Right before they end up with sharks circling them, having to make hard decisions about who's going to be eaten first."

"I'd let them eat me first," he says. "Because I'm a gentleman."

"That's so nice of you," I say. The farther I walk into the water, the colder it seems to get. I really hope we don't capsize. I don't think I could take it, being submerged in water this cold.

"Okay," Abram says. "Now listen. This is the important part of what we're doing."

"That makes me nervous," I say.

"We haven't done anything yet."

"No, just you saying that this is the important part. It feels like pressure. Like if I don't do it right, I'm going to end up as shark food."

"You're not going to end up as shark food," he says.

"Because there aren't any sharks around here?"

"No, because I would never let that happen."

"How are you going to save me from sharks?"

"You think I can't fight off a shark?"

"I'm not saying you *couldn't,* I'm just saying it's not a definite."

He holds the boat steady and looks at me. "Okay," he says. "Now, listen. We both have to get in at exactly the same time."

"How are we going to do that?" I have a vision of trying to vault myself into the boat and the whole thing just tipping over, with both of us falling into the water, flailing about. Actually, it would probably just be me flailing—Abram definitely doesn't seem like the flailing type.

"Carefully." Abram holds on to the boat and smiles at me, then counts off. "One . . . two . . . three . . ."

I hoist myself into the boat. It wobbles for a few seconds, including one second where I'm almost positive it's going to turn over, but then it rights itself.

"You okay?" Abram asks from the other side of the boat.

"Yeah," I say, shrugging. "No sweat."

We paddle farther out into the ocean, close enough so we can still see the kids splashing around on the shore, but far enough away that we have privacy. We pull the paddles back onto the boat and just sit there, floating lazily on the crystal clear water. The sun warms my face, and I close my eyes and take in a deep breath of ocean air, then let it out slowly.

When I open my eyes, Abram's staring at me.

"Sorry," I say, embarrassed. "I'm just not used to being out on the water."

"Don't apologize," he says, inching forward in the boat. He reaches out and puts his hand on my leg. "You look cute when you're trying to be peaceful."

"Trying?"

"Yeah." He moves even closer to me. "Isn't that what you were trying to do?"

"Be peaceful?"

He shrugs. "Yeah, or relax, whatever."

"I guess."

He brushes my hair back from my face, over my shoulders, then traces his finger over my jawline. "I can help you."

"Help me what?"

"Relax." He bends down and kisses my collarbone softly. His lips are warm and I shiver, remembering last night, his hands on my body, his weight on top of me as he moved into me slowly, stopping to whisper into my ear and ask if I was okay. He kisses me again now, this time moving up my neck. "Is it helping?"

I let my head fall back, enjoying the feel of his lips on my skin. "Yes," I say honestly. But as relaxed as I am, it's not the same as last night. I'm relaxed, yes, but not reckless. So even though it takes all my self-control, I pull away from him and scoot to the other side of the boat.

Abram groans. "Why are you moving all the way over there?"

"Because," I say, trying to sound flippant, "I want to talk."

"Okay," he says. "Let's talk." He moves a little closer.

"Nuh-uh," I say. "Stay where you are."

"For how long?"

"At least fifteen minutes of talking."

He laughs. "Fair enough."

I slide my hand down over the side of the boat and trail it along the water. "So do you like living here?" I ask.

"I love it," he says.

"And the club . . . you like working there?"

He nods. "Yeah. It's not a bad gig. I get to be out on the beach all day."

"Meeting girls."

He tilts his head. "You're even cuter when you're jealous."

"I'm not jealous!"

"You are."

"I'm not!"

"It's okay," he says, pretending to be serious. "I get it. I'm very in demand around here."

"I'll bet." I roll my eyes, but I'm not really joking. I know he said he doesn't usually do what he did with me last night, but how am I supposed to believe that? That he just met me and somehow found me so irresistible that he just *had* to take me home with him? It seems a little unlikely.

"No, but seriously," he says. "I like working there. My boss is cool and the money is good."

"Really?" I say. "You make a lot of money working there?"

"Well, it's relative," he says. "I make a lot of money for what it is. They give me a percentage of the door, which means I get a certain amount of money based on how many people I bring in. That alone is going to pay for my school next year."

"School?"

"Yeah." He nods. "I got into the University of South Florida, but I had to defer for a year because I couldn't afford it. But when I start next year, I'll be able to commute and keep my job at the club, too, which is great."

I nod. I feel my face turn red as I think about how I was complaining about not getting into Stanford, when I could pretty much go to any other school I wanted, and my parents would be able to pay for it.

"What are you going to major in?" I ask.

He shrugs. "I have no idea."

I smile. I love that he has no idea; I love that he's going to school close to home because he likes his life here and doesn't feel the need to search for anything else.

"You?" he asks.

"Me?"

"Yeah, what are you going to major in?"

"Something to do with science," I say. "At least, that was the plan. But now I really don't know."

He nods and dips a paddle back into the water, taking a second to straighten the boat out. "You know," he says. "Sometimes it's okay to not know what's going to happen. At least, in my humble opinion." He slides back across the boat toward me, and I have no choice but to meet him in the middle—I don't want to tip over. "You'll figure it out, Quinn," he says. "I know you will."

As he says the words, I believe him. He's comforting and exciting and wonderful all at the same time.

"Has it been fifteen minutes yet?" Abram asks.

"Probably not," I say.

But I let him kiss me anyway.

We spend the next hour paddling the boat around on the ocean, talking about everything and nothing.

Finally, just when I'm getting sunburned and hungry and we're about to head back to shore, Abram points. "Look," he says.

I turn to catch the tail end of a dolphin jumping out of the water before diving back in. "Oh!" I say, half-delighted, half-disappointed that I missed most of it. "Is he going to jump again?"

"He should," Abram says. "Keep watching."

I keep watching, hoping, and then a moment later, the dolphin appears again, followed immediately by another one. "Oh!" I say. "It's a family!"

"Yup," Abram says. "You see them a lot out here." But he sounds happy, and I'm not sure if it's because he's seeing the dolphins, or because he's happy that *I'm* seeing them.

"They're so beautiful," I say as we watch the dolphins pop up and down into the water.

Abram nods. "Yeah," he says. "It's a completely different thing when you see them out here in their natural environment. They're so free."

"Yeah." I hug my arms to myself, watching the dolphins.

Free.

Just the way I feel.

When we finally pull the boat back onto the beach, I'm tired and sweaty, but somehow invigorated at the same time. Being out on the ocean, the sun shining down on me, the salt water in my face and the wind in my hair, has left me feeling amazing.

As soon as I step onto the sand, Abram starts to dismantle his boat.

I just stand there watching him, totally in awe.

"You're folding up the boat," I say.

"Yeah." He grins.

"That's insane," I say, shaking my head, still not used to the idea that we were just out in the water, floating around on a fold-up canoe. I reach into my pocket and pull out my cell phone, which I'd put into a Ziploc to keep it from getting wet. The home screen is filled with messages.

Celia. Paige. Asking me where I am, telling me it was rude to just walk out of their room the way I did.

A text from my mom, asking me to please call her.

A bunch of missed calls from a number I don't recognize.

Another text from my mom, asking me to call her, that it's important.

One from my brother, telling me to call Mom, that she wants to talk to me, that it's important.

Something about the tone of the texts from my family makes my heart slide up into my throat. And that, coupled with the missed calls from the number I don't know, makes me instantly nervous. Is everything okay? Did something happen to my dad?

"Is everything okay?" Abram's asking.

"I'm not sure," I say. My hand is shaking as I go to call my mom back. "I have a bunch of texts from my family. I need to call my mom."

"Yeah, of course," he says, looking concerned.

I take a few steps away from him as I dial.

My mom picks up a second later.

"Quinn," she says.

"Mom," I say. "What's wrong? Is everything okay?"

"No, everything's not okay!" she says. But her voice sounds more exasperated and annoyed than sad or upset, and some of the tension flows out of my shoulders. "Where the hell have you been, young lady?"

"I was out on a boat with my friend," I say, before realizing that maybe I should have made up a lie. In my house, anything that's considered frivolous or fun isn't really an excuse—for anything. I can't even remember the last time my mom or dad did something just for fun. They're always working, and when they're not working, they're doing errands or projects around the house.

"Why didn't you answer your phone?" my mom demands. She sounds like it's the worst offense in the world, not answering your phone, when she's one of the hardest people to get ahold of in, like, the entire world.

"I just told you, I was out on a boat," I say.

"And you couldn't bring your phone?"

"No, I brought it, I just couldn't hear it." Seriously? Is she going to make me get into the nuances of wrapping your phone in a Ziploc bag and how that makes it almost impossible to hear or feel, even if you have it on vibrate?

"Okay," my mom says. "But please, Quinn, make sure to have your phone on you for the rest of your trip. You know your father and I worry."

They do? "Okay," I say. "Sorry." It's an automatic response. I didn't even do anything wrong—but she always makes me feel like I need to be apologizing.

"So I'm sure you must know by now that you haven't gotten into Stanford," she says.

"Yes," I say. "Um, I got an email."

"And that's why you've been avoiding me?"

"I wasn't avoiding you. I was just trying to come up with a plan." At least it's a half-truth. (A full truth if the plan was losing my virginity to a guy I just met, ha-ha.)

"Well, Daddy's making some calls," my mom says. "But the more important part, and the reason I'm calling you, is that I may have gotten you an internship this summer at Biogene."

"What?" My head is spinning, because she's throwing so much information at me that I'm having a hard time parsing it all out. Plus, a bunch of sorority girls have plopped down in the sand a few feet away and are giggling at each other while they take selfies. "Wait, I don't . . . what are you talking about?"

She sighs. "Quinn, can you please go somewhere where you can hear me?"

"I'm on the beach, Mom," I say. "I can't really get away." I move a couple more steps away from the college girls. "Okay, what were you saying about calls to Stanford?"

"What I was *saying*," my mom says, "is that your father

has made a few calls to Stanford."

"Yeah, I got that part. To who, though?"

"To Dr. Ellsbury and a few of his friends in admissions."

"Dad has friends in admissions?"

"Of course, Quinn, your father has friends everywhere at Stanford."

"Why didn't you mention this to me before?"

"Because there was no need for you to know before."

Her reasoning is confusing—why would she not want to tell me my dad had friends in admissions? Why would she let me think this whole time I'd been rejected, when she knew she could just have my dad make a couple of calls and it would all be fixed? And then I realize she *hadn't* let me think that—I never called her back after she sent me that text yesterday. But still. You'd think at some point during the whole application process she would have mentioned my dad being friends with people in the admissions department.

I'm not sure what's more depressing—that my mom didn't tell me so I would keep working hard, or that she actually has to use her connections now since I didn't live up to her expectations.

"What's he going to say to them?" I ask. I try to imagine the phone call. Will it be cut-and-dried, just a quick conversation? Or will he have to fly out there and wine and dine them first, take his friends out for a nice dinner and a round of golf before he can bring up the idea of his daughter getting into their school?

"He's going to tell them that there must have been a mistake, and ask if there's anything he can do to make them see what an asset you'd be to the university."

I know exactly what she's talking about. Money. My dad is going to offer to donate a ton of money to the university, maybe now, or maybe later, after they let me in. He's going to use his connections and his wealth to try to get me in, even though Genevieve in admissions specifically told me that there was no appeals process, that all their decisions were final.

I grip the phone in my hand. It's despicable, when you think about it, my dad using his position and money to break the rules. I think about all the other kids who didn't get in, the ones who've worked just as hard as I have. I think about them opening their rejection letters and having to tell their families they didn't get into Stanford. Those kids can't just have their dads make a phone call or write a check and have everything turned around.

It's not fair.

On the other hand, the thought that the whole Stanford thing might not be over, that I might be able to go there after all, is exciting. *I could go after all.* I'd be in California at this time next year, walking around Palo Alto with all my new college friends. And honestly, is my dad making a phone call really that bad? Isn't that how things work? I was willing to go to the interview at Biogene that my mom got me due to her connections. How is this any different?

"And what were you saying about the internship at Biogene?" I ask.

"The woman from Biogene left a message saying they filled it," my mom says. "So I got you an interview for another position. It's tomorrow at eleven o'clock, if you can be ready. It's a different woman in charge, but she can still meet you in downtown Sarasota. She's been trying to call you, but of course you haven't been answering."

I grip the phone even tighter. My stomach rolls when I think about how I didn't call my mom back yesterday. God, how *stupid* was I? Letting a dumb email I sent to myself when I was fourteen give me some kind of crazy breakdown that led me to LOSE MY VIRGINITY to a guy I don't even know and forget about everything else I have going on in my life? What the hell was I *thinking*? What if my mom had gotten me an interview for today? What if I hadn't been answering my phone, and I'd missed it?

Not to mention the fact that Celia and Paige are mad at me.

"Hello?" my mom says, sounding exasperated again. "Quinn, are you there?"

"Yes, I'm here," I say, all businesslike. "Can you text me the information for tomorrow's interview?"

"Yes."

"Thank you."

"And Quinn?" Her voice softens. "I want you to know that everything's going to be okay. I don't want you to worry about this, okay? We're going to take care of it. As a family."

"Thanks, Mom."

"You're welcome, Quinn."

We hang up the phone, and I just stand there, not moving, trying to process what just happened. Suddenly, everything blooms back into my life. Stanford. The internship. Everything I've ever wanted. But instead of feeling happy, I just feel . . . "defeated" isn't the right word. More like . . . empty. It's supposed to be exciting. And it is, at least a little bit. But not the way it's supposed to be. It's like a shiny penny that's been dulled. *It's fine,* I tell myself. *You're just surprised. It's going to take a little while for this to sink in.*

"Hey," Abram says as drops of cold water hit the back of my neck. I turn around to see him standing there on the sand, smiling, ocean water dripping from his fingers. He must have dipped his hand into the ocean and then flicked me with the cool salt water to get my attention. It has the desired effect—not only does he get my attention, but he shocks me out of my reverie. "Everything okay?" he asks when he sees my face.

"Yeah," I say. "Everything's great. Better than great, actually. That was my mom. She got me an interview with this biotech company tomorrow for an internship. And there might be a way I can go to Stanford after all."

"Wow," he says, sounding like he really means it. "That's awesome."

"Yeah."

But he must hear something in my tone, because he says, "Isn't it?" and he sounds kind of concerned.

I want to ask him if he thinks there's something wrong with the fact that my parents might be paying my way into a school I'm not even that excited about anymore, if he thinks it's weird they weren't even mad or disappointed, that they just immediately shifted into fix-it mode. My mom didn't even ask me how I felt about not getting in. She didn't even tell me what the new internship entails, or how she was able to get me an interview. It's easy to figure out, of course—either she knew someone, or she promised something to Biogene's drug reps, or . . . who knows. The reasons don't really matter.

"Quinn?" Abram asks. "Are you okay?" He's tilting his head, looking at me like he's worried.

For a split second, I want to tell him I'm not okay, that I don't know how I feel about any of this, that I have the sneaking suspicion my parents only wanted to get me into Stanford so they could look good to their friends, that as soon as it was something that affected them, they immediately started doing damage control. That maybe they should let me fight my own battles, that maybe not getting into

Stanford was just a lesson I needed to learn, that maybe it happened for a reason, that maybe if Stanford didn't want me, I should have just accepted it. I mean, what kind of message is it to send to your child that you can buy your way out of anything? What's going to happen when I get older? Are they going to keep bailing me out? Are they going to keep doing things like this for me? What if I don't have the kind of money they have? Are they teaching me not to work hard?

But I *have* worked hard. I've worked hard for four years, studying when I didn't want to, skipping out on things when my friends were off having fun. I joined clubs and extracurriculars that were awful, that ate up all my free time and left me feeling overwhelmed and depressed.

And since I've done all that, don't I at least deserve a chance? It's not my fault the system works this way. *Every* system can be manipulated, at least to some extent. It's why they ask on your application if you have any relatives who went to Stanford. It's why children of famous people score leading roles in movies or end up with hit songs. Do you really think Robin Thicke would be such a huge star if his father wasn't Alan Thicke? There's no way.

It's just the way of the world. And yes, I don't feel extremely excited about going to Stanford right now, but that's just because it's so new. I'd made my peace with the fact that I wasn't going. So of course it's going to take me a little while to adjust.

"Hello?" Abram asks. "Quinn?"

"Yeah," I say, shaking my head. "Sorry, I just..." I look into his eyes, at the way he's looking at me, and my heart squeezes.

Suddenly, I realize I need to get away from him. I can't think straight when I'm around him. He clouds my judgment—so much that he almost caused me to lose everything I've ever wanted.

"I have to go," I say.

He frowns. "You have to go?"

"Yeah, I need to get back to my hotel. I . . . I have my interview tomorrow, and I need to make sure I have something to wear." It's a lie. I know exactly what I'm going to wear—the gray Donna Karan suit that's folded neatly in my dresser, nestled next to one of those portable steamers so I can make sure I'm wrinkle-free. My mom packed the suit for me, making sure it was the last thing that went into my suitcase and double- and triple-checking I had it before I left.

"Okay," Abram says. "Well, can I take you to dinner later?"

"Sure," I say, even though I'm not sure at all.

"Do you want to meet at the Hub again? The place we ate last night? Like around six?"

"Sounds good." But even as I'm saying the words, I know I won't be there. He's bad for me. I've always known that, but now it's more apparent than ever, one of those huge truths that can't be ignored.

Abram takes a step toward me, and I can tell he's going

to kiss me. But at the last second, I move away.

"I'll see you later," I say.

I turn and start walking across the beach, my heart ripping into pieces and my eyes filling with tears.

*It's just hormones.*

*It doesn't mean anything.*

*You just met him.*

*He's bad for you.*

*Your feelings can't be real.*

I repeat the mantras over and over.

They don't make me feel better.

But I keep walking anyway.

Because if there's one thing I'm good at, it's self-discipline.

As I walk across the beach, my sadness starts to turn to anger and I kick at the sand, looking for someone or something to blame. Abram for being so charming. Celia and Paige for not stopping me when they knew I was doing something that was so obviously a bad idea. Lyla and Aven for making me write that stupid email in the first place.

My anger burns brighter, looking for a place to land. And then, almost like the universe has decided to serve me up the perfect target, I see Lyla lying on the beach. She's spread out on a towel next to Derrick. Derrick! So I guess they didn't break up after all. So then why was she with Beckett this morning? Is she cheating on Derrick? Are she and Beckett just good friends?

Who cares? I stomp across the sand toward where they're lying.

As I get closer, though, I realize I can't just start yelling at Lyla for making me write myself an email four years ago. I mean, that's totally insane. But I *can* yell at her for what she did to me this morning, just showing up like that at Abram's house when we're not even friends anymore. On some level I know I could also be *thanking* her for being worried enough to come looking for me, but I'm not thinking straight. I just want to yell at someone. So I do.

"What the hell were you thinking?" I shout as I get closer to her.

Lyla looks confused for a moment, and then she moves a little bit so the sun isn't in her eyes. "Oh, hi, Quinn," she says pleasantly.

"Don't 'oh, hi, Quinn' me," I say. "What the hell were you doing this morning?"

"This morning?" Derrick asks from the towel next to her. "What were you doing this morning?"

Oh, Jesus. So she *is* cheating on Derrick. So much for her being so judgmental about people doing the right thing and not making mistakes. My anger at her burns brighter, not just for making me send that email, not just for showing up at Abram's house this morning, but for cheating on her boyfriend, which is a totally scummy thing to do, and yet not forgiving me four years ago just because I did *one* thing wrong.

"Nothing," Lyla says quickly, sounding panicked.

Oh, for the love of god. How am I supposed to yell at her about this morning if I can't even bring it up in front of her boyfriend? Yes, we're not friends anymore, but still. I don't want to ruin her life by exposing her cheating scandal. It's none of my business.

"Can I talk to you alone?" I ask her.

Derrick puffs out his chest, like he's some kind of caveman and Lyla's his prehistoric wife. "Anything you can say to Lyla, you can say to me."

Ha!

"No." I shake my head emphatically. "I need to talk to her alone." I don't want to have to bring this up in front of Derrick, but if Lyla doesn't go with me, I might just have to. I'm feeling very reckless, like a teapot that's about to explode from all the pressure.

"Sure," Lyla says quickly, throwing on her cover-up. I start walking down the beach, glancing behind me to make sure she's following. When we're a few feet away from Derrick, I turn around and get ready to lay into her.

She looks nervous. Good. She should be nervous. I have a very biting tongue when I want to. But before I can decide what, exactly, I want to say, Lyla says, "Wanna go to the snack bar? I could use a soda."

Then I realize she's not nervous about my biting tongue, she's nervous about Derrick being close enough to overhear whatever it is I'm about to say to her. Which is silly, since we're definitely too far away for him to hear anything. And I don't *want* to go to the snack bar. I need to get back to my room and make sure I have everything ready for my interview tomorrow. I have to make sure I research the position, go over my notes, steam clean my suit! "Not really," I say.

Lyla rolls her eyes. "We're going."

Wow. She's acting pretty bratty and confident for someone who should be worried about me blowing up her spot.

But whatever. Fine. If she wants to choose the snack bar as the place where I yell at her, then I guess that's her prerogative. I start walking toward the main part of the beach, where the snack bar and the public bathrooms and showers are all housed in a huge pavilion. It takes me a second to realize Lyla's not following me. When I turn around to look behind me, she's just standing there on the sand, looking lost.

"Hello!" I say. "Are you coming or not?"

"Yeah," she says. "I'm coming." She rushes to catch up with me.

When we get to the snack bar, she gets in the line for food, which makes no sense. She actually wants to eat? I thought she just wanted to make sure she was away from Derrick when I started yelling at her for what happened this morning. But apparently not. Apparently she's hungry.

"What can I getcha?" the guy working the snack bar asks. He's way too chirpy for the kind of mood I'm in.

"Just a soda," I say, kind of rudely, even though he hasn't done anything wrong. But I don't want Lyla to get the idea that we're going to be hanging around here too long. She can get a drink and bring it right back to her spot on the beach when I'm done with her.

"Don't mind her," Lyla says to the guy. "She's kind of . . . uptight."

"No, I'm not!" I am so not uptight. Case in point: what I did last night.

Lyla orders a bag of chips and a soft pretzel. I guess she's not worried about what processed carbs and trans fats are going to do to her insides.

"So listen," I say when the snack bar guy goes to get our food. "I just wanted to tell you to please stop following me." I don't know why I say please. I mean, here I was, all set to yell at her, but now the wind has gone out of my sails. Something about her calling me uptight has kind of ruined the mood.

"I wasn't following you," she says. "Beckett said you might be in trouble, so I wanted to make sure you were okay. Excuse me for caring about you."

"Oh, right, like you just care about me so much." I roll my eyes.

"I wouldn't want anything bad to happen to you, if that's what you mean."

Wow. What a liar. "Really? Then why did you let me leave the room like that?"

"Like what?"

"Like I was going out to try and find a random guy to hook up with!" Does she not remember the fact that I came out of the bathroom dressed in a completely inappropriate outfit? Does she not remember that she asked me if I was okay, and that even though I obviously wasn't, she still let me go? I mean, talk about too little, too late. Showing up at Abram's house after we already slept together? God forbid something had happened to me. She would have been way too late.

"I'm not your keeper, Quinn," Lyla says. "I tried to say something, but you—"

The snack bar guy returns to the window. "That'll be sixteen dollars," he says happily.

"Sixteen dollars?" Lyla asks. She blinks. "For a bag of chips and a soda?"

"Well, and the pretzel," he says.

Lyla reaches into her cover-up and pulls out a crumpled-up ten-dollar bill. "I guess I'll put the chips back," she says sadly, like it's some big tragedy.

But she still doesn't have enough money. Without the

chips, it's twelve dollars. So then Lyla and the snack bar guy start getting into a fight over whether she can give the pretzel back, too. Apparently there's some health regulation that says you can't put pretzels back once they've been served. Which doesn't make any sense. The guy's wearing gloves. So who cares if he puts the stupid pretzel back?

So then Lyla says, fine, she'll keep the pretzel and put the *soda* back, but apparently she can't do that either because the soda's already been poured. Which makes more sense than the pretzel, because hello, obviously you can't put liquid back into a machine.

"Oh, for the love of god," I say, because I can't take listening to the two of them for one more second. I drop a ten-dollar bill onto the counter next to the one Lyla's already put there. "Here. Take it." How is it that I've somehow become responsible for paying for Lyla's unhealthy snacks? I came here to yell at her, not pay for her overpriced treats. It's actually kind of upsetting.

"Thank you," Lyla says politely.

The guy at the window seems annoyed, like he can't believe how stupid we are for not realizing how much things were going to cost. Which I guess makes sense. Lyla shouldn't have ordered so much food if she didn't have any money. Why did she go out on the beach with only ten dollars anyway? Doesn't she know any refreshments you buy on the beach are going to be crazy expensive?

Once Lyla's gathered up her food, she starts walking over to one of the picnic tables under the big stone pavilion. "Would you like a bite of pretzel?" she asks politely once we're sitting down.

"No." One, they're full of grease and fat. And two, I don't want to take anything from her.

"So what, exactly, do you want to say to me now?" she asks. "You already told me to leave you alone. So I'm leaving you alone. I won't chase you down at any other random guys' houses."

"Good," I say, thinking about telling her I won't be at any more random guys' houses, so she won't have to worry about it. But I don't. Let her think I might still be participating in scandalous hookups.

"Where'd you meet that guy anyway? He was seriously hot."

"At a club." Well, sort of. Technically we met on the beach. But I'm not going to tell Lyla that. I like her thinking of me out at a club, dancing and flirting.

"Really?" Lyla raises her eyebrows.

"Yeah. Why?"

"I dunno. It just doesn't seem like something you'd do."

"Yeah, well, you don't know me anymore." I'm saying it to hurt her, but she seems unfazed.

"Apparently not." She takes another bite of her pretzel. "You don't know me, either."

Obviously. Since she was cheating on her boyfriend. "Yeah, since you were cheating on your boyfriend," I say.

A flash of guilt passes across Lyla's face, but she recovers quickly. "I was not cheating on him! I told you, Beckett came to my room and told me you were in trouble."

"And since when are you such good friends with Beckett?" I can't help myself. I'm interested. I don't *want* to be interested, I don't want to be wondering what's going on in her life, why she was with Beckett when she's supposed to be with Derrick, why she just looked guilty if nothing is going on. But I can't help it.

"I'm not."

"Does Derrick know?" I press.

"Obviously not."

I shake my head and resist the urge to ask more. It doesn't matter. Like everything else in Lyla's life, it's none of my business. "Well, whatever. I don't have time to get caught up in your drama."

"*My* drama? You're the one who hooked up with some random guy."

I open my mouth to bite back with some smart retort, but then I change my mind. It doesn't matter. And besides, Lyla's kind of right. How can I judge her for possibly cheating on Derrick when the stuff I've done is just as scandalous?

"Sorry," Lyla says, and she sounds sincere. "I shouldn't

have said that. It's really none of my business."

It's the same thing I thought just a few moments ago. But something about *her* saying it hurts. I know it doesn't make any sense, but suddenly, I *want* it to be her business. I want her to be involved in my life, and I want to be involved in hers. I want to know what's going on with Beckett, and not because it's good gossip or because I want to hold it over her—I want to know because I miss her. And I want to be able to tell her about Abram, not because it will make me feel better, but because she's smart and she's caring and she's always given me really good advice. I want our business to be each other's because I miss her. A lot.

"Did you get the email?" I ask softly.

"The one we sent to ourselves? Yeah."

"Are you going to do what it says?" I ask. "Learn to trust?" That's what Lyla wrote to herself in the email she sent. *Before graduation, I will . . . learn to trust.*

She swallows hard and her face softens, like she's touched that I remembered what her email said, that I care enough to ask her about it. "Quinn . . . ," she says, and for one wonderful moment, I think she's going to tell me she wants to be friends again, that she misses me, that she forgives me, that whatever happened in the past is in the past, that we can forget about it, or even if we can't *completely* forget about it, that we can at least *talk* about it, that we can figure it out.

But the silence stretches on, until I realize she's not going to say anything. And when it becomes apparent that she doesn't care as much as I do, my heart closes up.

"Never mind," I say, standing up. I can't believe how stupid I was to think there was even a chance she might care about being friends again. "Just stay out of my life, okay?"

And then I turn around and walk away.

# TWELVE

I NEVER MEANT TO TELL LYLA'S SECRET.

It wasn't something I did on purpose, to ruin her life or make her feel bad. In fact, at the time I did it, I had no idea it was going to alter the course of our friendship so drastically. If I had, I never would have said anything.

On one of the first Wednesdays of our sophomore year, Lyla announced to Aven and me that her parents were getting divorced. She seemed okay with it—her parents hadn't been getting along, and she didn't even see her dad that much. But a couple of weeks later, while they were shopping at the mall, Lyla told Aven her dad had asked her to come and live with him. (I wasn't there because I was doing volunteer work on a political action committee—another way that my Stanford obsession was messing with my life.)

Later that same day, Aven came to my house to spend the night, and she told me what Lyla had said about her

and his invitation. Usually, Lyla would have been at
my house, too, but she didn't come that night because she
said she didn't want to leave her family, with everything that
was going on. It was weird, because Lyla kept insisting to
us that she was fine with her parents' divorce, that her parents hadn't been close for a while, that she hardly saw her
dad anyway, and so the fact that he was moving out didn't
change anything. She said it was business as usual at her
house, that her parents weren't fighting, that the vibe there
wasn't even any more tense than it usually was.

But she didn't come to my house that night. I thought
maybe Lyla just needed some time alone to process things,
until Aven told me about how Lyla's dad had asked her to
move with him to New Hampshire.

Aven and I were upset at the prospect of losing our best
friend, so we ordered pizza and discussed the best way to
handle the situation. We'd be devastated if Lyla moved away,
but we decided we couldn't let our emotions stand in the
way of what was best for her.

We'd support her. If she needed to go, we'd be the best
friends ever. We'd help her pack her stuff and take a bus to
New Hampshire after she moved to help her set up her room.

"What if she makes new friends?" Aven had asked, taking a sip of her orange soda.

"Of course she'll make new friends," I'd said. "But they
won't be friends like us." I knew it was silly to think that

Lyla wouldn't make friends at her new school—of course she would. But I couldn't fathom the idea that they'd be as close to her as Aven and I were. The three of us were *best* best friends—the kind who were more like sisters, the kind you could call any time of the day or night, the kind you could have fun with even when you were doing nothing. I could count on Aven and Lyla more than I could count on my own family. They knew me. They *saw* me. They understood me.

"Yeah," Aven said thoughtfully. She scraped the cheese and toppings off her pizza with her fork and then deposited them on my plate, knowing I would want them without even having to ask. I scooped them up onto my slice. "But what if she forgets about us?"

"She won't," I said, picking up my double-toppinged pizza and biting into it. "We'll make an effort. We'll take buses to see her, we'll beg for rides. And in a year we'll have our licenses and then it won't matter—we'll get to see her whenever we want."

This seemed to settle Aven down. "Don't say anything to anyone," she said. "I don't think Lyla wants anyone but us to know."

"Of course."

We spent the rest of the night watching movies and eating Ben & Jerry's. I think about how naive I was back then, how I thought that nothing could come between the three of us. But the reality was that just a few days later Lyla wasn't speaking to me, she wouldn't return my texts or my calls, she wouldn't even look at me when she passed me in the halls at school.

But that night, at least, I wasn't super concerned. I was worried about Lyla, of course, but I wasn't *mad* at her for not telling me, or for wanting to move in with her dad. I was sad she might be moving away, yes—but I loved Lyla. She was my best friend (along with Aven), and all I wanted was for her to be happy. And not in that fake way where people say they want the other person to be happy while secretly judging them for everything they're doing. I really, truly wanted her to be happy.

I wasn't even annoyed at Lyla for confiding in Aven about her possible move before she told me. I knew at some point she would tell me—she just hadn't gotten around to it yet. That was the amazing thing about the friendship I had with them—there was never a feeling that two of us were closer than the three of us, no feeling of being left out ever. I knew that kind of thing was rare—I'd been involved in enough middle school friendships and seen enough from the outside to know that girls can be ruthless, and when you're in a threesome, most of the time someone is going to get left out. But it was never like that with us.

Anyway, when Aven left the next morning, I *was* thinking about Lyla, but only because I was worried about her. I knew that even though she said she was fine, she must have been feeling at least a little weird, since she'd skipped our sleepover in favor of staying home with her family. I thought about calling her, but I didn't want to push it. I didn't want her to feel like I was forcing her to talk about things before she was ready.

So I brewed myself a coffee and sat down at my dining room table and did what I always did when I wanted to avoid thinking about something that was going on in my life—I lost myself in schoolwork.

I pulled out my math book and started doing the practice problems our teacher had given us for review. It was kind of a joke—math was (and still is) my best subject, and the problems on the review sheets were always the exact same problems that were on the tests. I guess our teacher figured most kids wouldn't do the review sheets, and so if they did, she'd give them a bit of a reward.

I always did the review sheets, not because I needed the practice, but because I liked knowing the problems that were going to be on the test. If I got one wrong on the review sheets (the answer key was in the back of our textbook), I could just make sure I corrected it. Then I would memorize all the problems and the solutions, and just make sure to do it right on the test.

It was a fabulous system that had earned me a one hundred average in math. (It was actually above a one hundred, because I'd done a bunch of extra-credit sheets, but you couldn't get more than a one hundred, obviously. But whatever.)

Anyway, there I was, my math book open in front of me, trying to forget about Lyla and hoping she would call me. I kept checking my phone, hoping I'd have a text from her, or at least from Aven, letting me know that she'd talked to her and that she was okay.

But there was nothing.

I started to feel restless, and even my math problems couldn't calm me down.

I wandered into the living room to see what Neal was doing, but he'd fallen asleep on the couch in front of CNN. I picked up the remote and made a big bunch of noise turning off the TV in an effort to wake him up, but he didn't budge.

Finally, I wandered outside to where my parents were working on their organic garden. They were trying to sell our house, and they'd gotten it into their heads that an organic garden was going to add value to the property. Updated bathrooms and granite countertops with a marble backsplash weren't enough for them. Someone had told them that organic gardens were the new "it" thing. And apparently getting the garden started was a huge pain in the ass, so if your house already had one, well, then it would be very in demand.

"Hey," I said, when I got to the corner of the backyard where they were working. "What are you guys doing?"

"Just starting some seedlings," my mom said, like it was totally normal to be planting a garden you had no interest in actually taking care of or using.

"Isn't it a little too cold to be planting a garden?" I asked.

"We're not planting into the ground, Quinn," my mom said, like she was some kind of agricultural expert. "We're planting them in pots and putting them under a light in the garage. We'll let them grow all winter, then transfer them outside when it gets warmer. Spring is the best time to put your house on the market."

"Oh. Okay." I didn't care that we were moving. We never left the school district, so it wasn't like I had to worry about changing schools, and if I didn't like the house, it didn't really matter, because we'd be moving again soon. I still had boxes of stuff in my closet at this house that I hadn't even unpacked. What was the point? We'd just be leaving before I had a chance to use anything anyway.

"Now it says here we need to churn the soil," my dad said. He was reading off his iPad. Normally I would question how successful this garden was going to be if they were starting it based off internet directions, but if there was one thing I knew about my parents, it was that when they put their minds to something, they usually made it happen.

"Can you go get more from the garage?" my mom asked.

My dad scurried off, and my mom turned to me. "Would you like to help?"

I wasn't much for physical labor, then or now, but I had nothing better to do. Plus—and this is the embarrassing part, the part that makes me wonder if maybe I, at least on some level, *did* tell Lyla's secret on purpose—I didn't often get a chance to spend that much time alone with my mom.

Yes, we did things as a family—benefits at the hospital, meals out, ski vacations in Europe, drives to New York for dinner and a show when my mom felt like "relaxing." But my mom and I never really did anything alone. We never just decided to have a girls' night, to pull up a chick flick on Netflix and eat ice cream, or pop over to the mall to shop for summer dresses and cheap shoes. If I needed an outfit for something, my mom gave me her credit card and I went with Aven and Lyla.

That's not to say my mom ignored me—she always asked me about school and what was going on in my life. But I never felt like there was anything special about our bond as mother and daughter. She had the exact same kind of relationship with me as she had with Neal. And it wasn't that I wanted to be her favorite—I just wanted to feel like we had something the rest of the family couldn't understand, the way my dad and Neal could discuss soccer and whether a Porsche was better than a Ferrari.

"Start pouring soil into these pots," my mom said.

I picked up the bag. It was heavy, but it got lighter as I went, and I fell into a nice rhythm, pouring soil into pots, filling them up almost to the top.

"How's school?" my mom asked.

"Good."

"Were you studying for math?"

I nod.

"Review sheets?"

I nodded again.

I waited for her to ask me if anything was wrong. I don't know why I expected she would—maybe because I was working on a house project with her, which she knew was one of my least favorite things to do. She'd finally stopped asking me to help after I pointed out the fact that she should just hire someone to do all the things she wanted done. I think I'd hit a nerve about her need to control and her need to always have something to do.

We worked in silence for a few more minutes, me pouring dirt into pots, her spraying the hose to moisten the soil when I was done. Finally, I couldn't take it anymore.

"So Lyla's parents are getting divorced," I blurted.

"Oh, that's too bad," my mom said. She didn't sound surprised. In her world of being a doctor, divorces were part of the job description—doctors worked long hours, they were never home, they might have to take off in the middle of the night to go save a life. And god forbid you married someone during their residency, or when they were in med school—those marriages were almost certain to fail. As a result, when my mom heard about a divorce, she was able to be almost completely unemotional about it.

"Yeah," I said. "It is."

"Is Lyla okay?" my mom asked.

I looked up in surprise. It was such an unexpected question—my mom didn't inquire about emotions, not mine, and certainly not my friends'. It was something I'd grown to accept about her. Her father, my grandpa, wasn't much on talking, and before he died my only memory of him was a meal where he was sitting at the head of a dining room table, telling everyone to be quiet. I was four. We sat there, and I ate my dinner in complete silence.

"I don't know," I said. "I haven't talked to her."

My mom nodded and moved the spray of water over the pot I'd just finished filling.

"She got invited to move in with her dad," I said, not because I was even that upset about it, but because I'd sensed an opening. "In New Hampshire."

"Is she going?"

"I think so," I said. "But I'm really not sure."

"You'll miss her," my mom said. "But New Hampshire is certainly close enough for lots of visits."

"Yeah."

My dad came back with more soil then, and that was the end of the conversation. I didn't think anything of it. I wasn't telling my mom because I wanted to talk about Lyla, or because I was upset she was moving. I did it because I was looking for some kind of connection.

And that would have, should have, could have, been the end of it.

Until my mom ran into Lyla's mom at Whole Foods, and they started talking, and my mom made a comment about how if Lyla's mom needed any antianxiety pills, she should make an appointment to come to see her, and that having a child leave the house and move with their father to another state must be extremely stressful.

But of course, Lyla's mom didn't know anything about Lyla moving to New Hampshire. Because it wasn't even a real plan. It was just something that was being discussed. So Lyla's mom flipped out, and then she went home and told Lyla, and by the time I saw Lyla again at school, she was irate. At me, for telling my mom. And at Aven for telling me.

The three of us got into it outside before first period, so badly that I was afraid it might come to a fistfight. But even though I knew Lyla was really mad—it was the worst fight we'd had since we'd been friends—I thought the whole thing was going to end up flaming out. I figured it was kind of like a bomb—it had gone off, and now we'd pick up the pieces, talk about it, and move on.

But it wasn't like that.

Lyla shut down. Completely.

She wouldn't talk to me or Aven. I tried texting her a

bunch of times, but she didn't want to hear my apologies. I tried to explain it to her, to tell her that that if I'd known my mom was going to run into her mom, I never would have said anything. But Lyla didn't care.

Looking back, I think she'd taken the anger she felt toward her dad for making her choose between her parents, and toward her mom for being such a mess that she couldn't deal with Lyla not living with her for a while, and put it onto Aven and me.

But I still felt horrible. *Why* had I told my mom? Aven had asked me not to tell anyone, and even though I didn't really consider my mom someone of importance, I'd still told. I'd broken my promise, and I felt awful.

At first, Aven and I worked together to make sure Lyla would talk to us again. But when it started to become clear that Lyla wasn't going to just get over it, Aven started resenting me. She never said it, but I think deep down, she blamed me for what had happened. Aven and I started slowly drifting apart, and after a while, we drifted completely apart.

I'd never felt more alone in my life. So I did what I always did when things got hard—I threw myself into my work. Extra credit, extra responsibilities, volunteering, committees, meetings . . . now that I had no friends, I had no need for free time, so I was able to pack my schedule with things that would look good to Stanford.

And after about six months, I met Celia while working at

the food pantry. We bonded over our Ivy League ambitions, and she introduced me to Paige, who was working there, too. They invited me to a party that night, to blow off steam after our long day of being on our feet handing out food. I usually avoided parties like the plague, opting instead for sleepovers with Lyla and Aven, or nights out to the mall or the movies. But obviously I hadn't been doing any of that, and so my lack of socialization made me desperate enough to say yes.

And that was it. I slid into Celia and Paige's threesome, not because I was all that suited for it, but because I was hungry for a group to be in.

And after a while, Lyla and Aven started to fade from my memory.

# THIRTEEN

WHEN I GET BACK TO THE HOTEL AFTER TALK-
ing to my mom and leaving Abram and Lyla on the beach, I
head right for Celia and Paige's room. I'm in full-on damage-
control mode now, and I need to make up with them. I
mean, what the hell was I thinking, blowing them off for
some guy? It's completely humiliating and totally against
every girl code in the book. I almost threw away my friendships, my future, *everything* for some guy I didn't even know.
I flush as I think about the fact that I lost my virginity to
him. I slept with him. I had sex with him! I might be able to
make up with Celia and Paige, but I'm never going to be able
to change that.

But I'm not going to think about that right now. I just
need to focus on one thing at a time. Almost like a to-do list.
One, make up with Celia and Paige. Two, get my outfit ready
for tomorrow's interview. Three, figure out if there's any way

I can help my parents get me into Stanford. Maybe I can write a special statement, or ramp up my volunteer work, or send updated transcripts showing I've kept my grades up and haven't gotten senioritis like a lot of kids at my school.

Of course I know the only thing that's *really* going to get me into Stanford is my dad writing a check or making them some kind of promise, but it still makes me feel a little better to think there might be *something* I can do.

When I get to Celia and Paige's room, I pause before knocking, trying to figure out what I'm going to say to the two of them. Finally, I decide to just keep it simple. Apologize. Say I'm sorry. Explain that I didn't mean to hurt them, that I just got caught up in a boy and the thrill of it all.

*But you didn't just get caught up in a boy. You really liked him. And you didn't want to stay and take care of Celia when she was drunk—you've never really wanted to do that.*

I hesitate. But then I tell myself those thoughts are coming from the part of me that wants to take the easy way out. My feelings for Abram are based on nothing but hormones and vacation and stupid teenage lust. They don't have anything to do with Abram himself. And this whole thing with Celia and Paige—yes, I didn't want to stay and take care of Celia, but some of that was motivated by wanting to go see Abram. Which was based on hormones and vacation and stupid teenage lust. It's a vicious cycle.

I knock on the door, hoping they'll be there.

"Come in!" Celia opens the door without even asking who it is. I get nervous for a second that they're not going to accept my apology, that maybe they'll say they've realized they can't count on me and so they're just . . . done with me. I know that's crazy. It wasn't like I did anything horrible to them. But then I have a flashback to standing outside school that day, Lyla yelling at me and Aven, the two of us just standing there, helpless.

Celia sits at the desk chair, one of those plug-in lighted magnifying mirrors in front of her. Paige stands behind her, holding strands of long blond hair extensions.

"You need to place them perfectly," Celia is instructing. "It's really important, because if you don't, they're going to slip. And if they slip, everyone's going to be able to see the tops of them, and that, like, defeats the purpose. You know, of people thinking they're real."

"Okay," Paige says, not sounding that sure.

The two of them have full faces of makeup on, way too much for daytime, so I'm assuming they're getting ready for something.

"Hi," I say.

"Hi," Celia says stiffly.

Paige doesn't say anything. She just clips an extension onto Celia's head.

"Good!" Celia says, turning her head and admiring Paige's work. "Good job, Paige!" Paige beams, and a flash of annoyance pulses through me. Why does Paige have to do everything Celia says? And why does she need Celia's approval so much? And over something so trivial and demeaning as putting in hair extensions? Why couldn't Celia put in her own damn hair extensions?

"I see you're feeling better," I say, making sure my voice stays upbeat.

"You know I recover quickly," Celia says. It's true. She's always having little drunken mishaps and feeling sick, but after she eats something and takes a quick nap, she's usually fine. Last year she got drunk on the field trip to Conifer Lake, puked in the bushes and everything, and by the time Paige got her a honey bun and Celia took a nap on the bus home, she was able to finish the rest of the school day like it was nothing.

"Yeah." I clear my throat. "Listen," I say. "I'm not . . . I'm sorry about what happened earlier."

Celia gets quiet, takes a deep breath through her nose, then swivels around in her chair and looks at me. Paige sets the hair she's holding down on the desk and turns to look at me, too. I see her eyes flick to Celia's face, trying to figure out what Celia's going to say. And I get it—Celia is the one in charge of this. If Celia says I'm forgiven, then Paige will follow suit. If Celia decides she's still mad, then so is Paige.

"Go on," Celia says patiently.

"I just got confused for a little while," I say. "I was just really . . ." I trail off, because now that she's put me on the spot, I don't know what exactly it is I'm sorry for. Is it because I didn't want to hang out with them? Because I didn't want to order Celia's pizza? I'm not really sorry for those things. But I can't say that. There's no way Celia's going to want to hear about how I'm sick of taking care of her.

It's not that bad, I tell myself. She's a good friend. So what if she's a little bit spoiled? She's been there for me when I had no one. And if I blow her off just because she can be a little entitled, isn't that exactly like what Lyla did to me, by just giving up on a friendship after one fight?

"You were just really . . . ," Celia prompts.

"I just really got worked up over Abram," I say. "He's really good-looking, and it was fun getting attention. So I kind of got, like, caught up in him." I try to convince myself the words are true—maybe if I say them enough, I'll start to believe them.

Celia nods, like she can accept this. "Okay," she says. "I mean, I understand."

"Me too," Paige says kindly. "I know you don't get that much attention from guys. So it would make sense you kind of freaked out."

"So can we just move on?" I ask, feeling my fists clench at my side. It's actually better to move on, and the faster the better, because if I have to sit here and explain myself to them for one more second, I'm pretty sure we're going to get into another fight.

"Yes," Celia says. She jumps up from her chair and envelops me in a hug.

And after a moment, Paige does the same.

They don't ask me any questions about losing my virginity. I don't think it's because they don't care, although that could be a small part of it. They're doing it mostly because they want to make it clear they're still mad at me, that they're not going to go out of their way to show an interest in my life or be super nice to me right away. In their opinion, I messed up, and I'm going to have to prove myself again, at least for a little while.

On the other hand, they're getting ready for a sunset cruise around the key, and they just assume I'm going with them. I kind of have to, since (a) I don't want them to be mad at me anymore, and (b) I need something to do, especially since I'm not going to be meeting Abram.

Abram. Whenever I think of him, emotion flows through my body like a wave. But I push him out of my mind and focus on getting ready for the cruise. When I think of sunset cruises, I think of people getting dressed up in semi-nice clothes and being served a fancy dinner consisting of exquisite-sounding seafood dishes, like mussels in garlic butter with truffle oil. But Celia quickly sets me straight when I come out of the bathroom wearing a simple red T-shirt dress.

"No," she says, shaking her head. "You can't wear that. It's not sexy enough."

She's changed into a black glittery miniskirt and a hot-pink top that ties behind her neck and hits just below her belly button. Paige is in a red bandeau dress with straps that crisscross in the back and show off her tanned skin.

"You can borrow this," Paige says, holding up a pair of short shorts and a tuxedo-style tank top.

Celia nods. "Very fashion forward," she says. "And those shorts will look killer with your legs."

I reach out and take the clothes, thinking of how ridiculous they're going to look on me. It's definitely not an outfit I would ever choose for myself, even if I decided I wanted to go for a sexier look. This isn't last night, when I was pretending to be something I'm not.

*Abram.*

I glance over at the clock.

Two minutes after six.

I should be meeting him now.

I wonder if he's at the restaurant, waiting for me, wondering where I am, if he's worried about me or if he knows he's being stood up. The desire to be there with him is so overwhelming that for a moment, my eyes fill with tears.

"Jesus, Quinn, you don't have to cry about it," Celia says,

sounding annoyed. "If you want to wear a T-shirt, go ahead and wear it."

"It's not a T-shirt," I say. "It's a T-shirt dress."

"Whatever," Celia says.

"It's a nice color," Paige says, deciding to show me a little sympathy. "It's nice for a sunset cruise."

"Thanks," I say. I turn around and head back into the bathroom, blinking back the tears that are threatening to spill down my cheeks.

*Stop being pathetic,* I tell myself. *He's just a boy you barely know. You're only feeling this way because you feel guilty about standing him up, and because you had sex with him.*

I know better than to think sex means anything. Just because you sleep with someone doesn't mean you have a connection. In fact, it's just your body tricking you into *thinking* you have a connection. Especially for girls. It's, like, a scientific fact that once a woman has sex with someone, a hormone gets secreted in her body that makes her feel like she's in love with the person she just slept with.

It's not real. It's just biology.

And Abram's a big boy—I'm sure he can handle the fact that he's been stood up. He's probably not even worried about it. He's probably already moved on. I picture him standing there by the hostess stand, waiting for me, and then when it becomes obvious that I'm not coming, walking down the beach, stopping to talk to whatever sorority girls or vacationers in bikinis happen to be around. His parents are probably still out of town. Maybe he'll take one of those girls back to his house tonight, the same way he did with me.

"Quinn!" Paige calls. "Are you almost ready?"

"Yeah," I say, pushing the thoughts of Abram out of my head once again. "Just a second."

"I'm going to hook up with someone tonight," Celia says. The sunset cruise takes off from a different part of the key than the one we're staying on—it's only about a mile or so away from the hotel, but there was no way Celia was going to make it there in the shoes she's wearing. Paige, either, really. She still has blisters from last night.

Plus, even though it's six o'clock, the humidity is killer. We would have been sweating by the time we got to the dock, and I don't think that would have been good for Celia's hair extensions. She's very worried about them. She keeps reaching up and touching them nervously, like she's afraid they're going to come out at any moment. I hope whoever she hooks up with doesn't end up running his fingers through her hair. He might end up with a surprise.

Anyway, the three of us are smushed into the back of a pedicab on our way to the other side of Siesta Key. It's kind of awkward, sitting here while some guy works his ass off to haul us to a sunset cruise, but Celia and Paige thought it would be so fun riding in a pedicab! Which it so totally isn't. Every time we go over a bump, it feels like we're going to tip over.

"Who?" Paige asks. "Who will you hook up with?"

"Someone on the party cruise," Celia says.

"What party cruise?" I ask.

Celia pats her hair. "The party cruise we're going on. Right now. Hello?"

Paige shakes her head at me. "You're still being kind of weird."

"I thought you said this was a sunset cruise," I say.

"It is," Celia says. "A sunset party cruise."

I sigh. A sunset party cruise is a lot different from a sunset cruise. A sunset cruise means dinner and standing on the deck (bow? stern?), watching the sun go down. A sunset *party* cruise means drinking and boys and standing in a corner while Celia and Paige grind on random guys. I'm so not in the mood for any of that.

*You're only in the mood to be with Abram right now.*

The pedicab goes over another bump. I decide to take it as a sign that I shouldn't be thinking about Abram. Kind of like one of those negative reinforcements where you snap a rubber band against your wrist every time you think of something you don't want to think about, and then eventually, you stop thinking about whatever it is because you start associating it with pain.

"Sir, can you please be careful!" Celia screeches to the driver, an older man with sunburn on the bald part of his head. "We really need to get there in one piece."

I'm not sure if he can hear Celia, but if he does, he doesn't acknowledge her. Not that I blame him. I mean, the man is hauling three entitled girls down to a sunset party cruise during their senior trip. If I were him, I wouldn't give a shit about jostling us around, either.

When we finally get to the harbor and climb out of the pedicab, Celia pays the guy, shaking her head the whole time. When she's not looking, I make sure to give him an extra ten dollars for a tip and thank him profusely. Not that he did that great of a job—we almost got hit by cars a few times, and after Celia yelled at him, he made sure to go over every single bump full force. But still.

We walk up the boardwalk to the boat, where we're once again ID'd before being let on. But this time Celia doesn't even try to convince the person working the door that she should get a stamp saying she can drink. One, because the person taking our money is a girl, and Celia knows her charms work better on men, and two, because she's obviously learned it doesn't matter if she has a stamp or not. She'll be able to find some pathetic guy to get her whatever she wants.

The actual boat is nothing like I pictured it. I thought it would be one of those high-end yacht-type boats, with round tables covered with white tablecloths and a nice buffet and beverage station in the corner. Of course, that was before I knew it was a party cruise. I wonder what it says about me that I'd rather be on a cruise set up for forty-year-olds instead of one that's for people my age. Probably that I'm boring.

The boat is filled with people already, crowded onto the deck, dressed in various stages of nothingness. Seriously, there are girls here wearing nothing but bikinis. Why would you come on a cruise wearing a bathing suit? It's not like we're going to be swimming.

There's a DJ pumping electronica on one of the upper decks, and I can feel the beat of the music vibrating through my body. The actual inside, main part of the boat is a little less congested. There's a buffet table filled with appetizers against one wall and a small bar in the corner, where two female bartenders wearing yellow crop tops and tight denim shorts are mixing up drinks.

"Let's get virgin daiquiris," Celia says. "That way guys will think we already have alcohol and they'll be more willing to buy us some."

"Since when have you had any problems getting guys to buy you drinks?" I ask. Guys don't care that she's underage. They like buying her alcohol—it makes them feel like they're big and important.

"I don't," Celia says, an edge in her voice. I see her eyes

flick out to the deck of the boat, and I know she's sizing up the competition. There are a lot of pretty girls out there, and a lot of good-looking guys. Not the kind of scene she's used to. I bite back a smile at the fact that she's kind of worried about it. I know it's not that nice, but I kind of like seeing Celia insecure.

I order my daiquiri first, and sip it as I wait for Celia and Paige to get theirs.

And that's when I see him.

Abram.

He's out on the deck, sitting on the long bench that wraps around the perimeter of the boat, his face obscured by a guy in a khaki shorts who's standing in front of him. In fact, it's so obscured that at first I'm not sure if it's even him. But then the guy in khaki shifts just a little bit, and I get a perfect view.

*Abram.*

It's definitely him. I watch, my stomach turning inside out, as a girl wearing a strapless maxi-dress sits down next to him and starts to flirt. I look away before I can see if he smiles back at her. I feel like a dagger has been pushed into my heart.

What is he doing here? He's supposed to be with me, taking me out to dinner, walking on the beach with me. And instead he's on this party cruise, talking to some girl. A day after he had sex with me! Wow. Just wow.

"This tastes good without alcohol," Paige says, sipping her daiquiri.

Celia rolls her eyes, like she can't believe how stupid Paige is for thinking that.

But I'm barely even listening. The guy in the khakis has moved back in front of Abram and the girl, and it's making me anxious. Suddenly, I want to see what's going on.

"I'll be right back," I say to Paige and Celia before I can stop myself. They don't answer, mostly because I'm pretty sure they don't hear me. Instead, they've started talking to some guys at the bar—Celia's giggling and patting at her extensions.

I turn and start making my way through the crowd. I just want to get a better look at him, to see what he's doing, but there are so many people that it's almost impossible to move. When I'm finally able to get a clear view of where he was sitting, he's gone. The girl in the maxi-dress is also nowhere to be found—instead, there are a couple of girls in white bikinis sitting there, taking selfies.

I wonder if Abram went somewhere with that girl, if they're making out in a dark corner, if he's going to bring her home tonight and take her out to breakfast tomorrow. I know I was thinking that could be a possibility when I stood him up, that I even used those thoughts to make myself feel better, but now, being faced with him flirting with another girl right in front of me, it's too much to bear.

I need to get off this boat.

I start pushing through bodies, not even bothering to say excuse me or find the best route. I just plow through, stepping on feet, shoving at hips and arms, until finally, I'm almost at the exit. But just when it's in sight, the girl working the door puts one of those hook ropes across the dock, blocking it. A second later, the boat starts to move away from the shore.

"Wait," I say. "Please, wait, I need to get off the boat." But no one can hear me, because at that moment, a huge cheer goes up from the crowd. The music rises in volume, and the ship starts to move faster.

I lean over the railing, taking deep breaths, in and out, in and out, until finally, my heart rate starts to slow.

*Okay*, I tell myself, *this is not the end of the world*. I can certainly survive a few hours on a boat with Abram. Three hours. That's all it is. Three hours until I can go back to the hotel and never have to see him again. I can certainly get through three hours. And if I can't, well, then I really had no business sleeping with him in the first place. If you're mature enough to have sex, you should be mature enough to handle the consequences of that sex, i.e., seeing the guy you had sex with flirting with someone else.

And honestly, how hard is it going to be to avoid him? There are a ton of people here. I'll just hang out in a corner somewhere and make sure I don't run into him. Maybe I'll even tell Celia and Paige what's going on. They'd love to get all self-righteous and protect me from Abram. Especially Celia. One time at Hattie Gardner's sweet sixteen, Celia spent the whole time bringing hors d'oeuvres over to Paige's table after Cody Carlisle invited Paige to be his date and then showed up with Regan Lewis. You know Celia thought it was a big deal if she was actually waiting on someone.

Feeling better, I decide to go back to the bar and find my friends.

But as soon as I turn around, there he is.

Again.

Abram.

Standing in front of me, his hands in his pockets, looking at me with that intense gaze of his, the same one he was giving me last night when we were together.

I freeze.

And then, after a long moment, he starts walking toward me.

"I'm glad to see you're okay," he says, pretending to look me up and down. "No bruises, no bumps, no illnesses."

"What?" I ask, confused. I'm thrown by his presence, by his closeness, and I'm having a hard time focusing on what he's saying.

"Just glad you're okay," Abram repeats, shrugging. "When you didn't show up at the restaurant I thought, you know, Quinn must have had an emergency, she's not the type of girl to just stand me up. And it's not like she could have called me, because she doesn't have my number." He pauses, waiting for me to say something, but I don't. "Of course, then I remembered I gave my number to your friend, and so if you had *really* wanted to get in touch with me, you could have."

"Abram . . . ," I start.

"No, it's okay." He shakes his head. "I get it. You were just using me."

"*Using* you?" I repeat, shocked. "No, I wasn't!"

"Please, Quinn," he says. "You came out last night looking for trouble. You thought you'd have a night of fun, sleep with a local boy, and then head back home and not have to worry about any of the fallout, right?"

"No." I shake my head. "That's not how it was at all."

"Then how was it?"

"It was . . ." I think about it. Is he right? Was I just using him? I'd gone out to that club on a mission—I wanted to have an adventure, to do something out of my comfort zone. And I zeroed in on him and made him part of that plan without even consulting him. I never stopped to think that maybe he wouldn't be too excited to just have sex with me and then never talk to me again. I thought he wouldn't care. But why? Because he's a guy? Because it seemed like that kind of thing happened to him all the time?

"Wait a minute," I say now. "What are you doing here?"

"I waited for you for a half hour," he says, and shrugs. "And then one of my friends invited me to go on the cruise, so I decided to come."

"And what about the girl in the hot-pink dress?" I ask, desperate to somehow turn this back around on him.

"What girl?" he asks, confused.

"The girl I just saw you flirting with! Did she invite you here, too?"

"I wasn't flirting with anyone," he says. "That girl sat down next to me, and then I saw you, and I came to find you and figure out why you stood me up." Even though he doesn't come right out and ask, I can tell he's waiting for some kind of explanation. He's hoping something really *did* come up, that I didn't just blow him off to go on some party cruise with my friends—friends he knows I don't even like that much.

"Abram . . . ," I start. "It's just . . . it's complicated." My eyes fill with tears again, and I don't trust myself to say anything more.

He takes a step closer to me, his arms encircling my waist and pulling me toward him. "It's okay," he says. "Whatever it is, Quinn, it's okay. You can tell me, we can figure it out."

I lean my head against his chest, feeling his arms around me, remembering what it felt like last night, lying close to him, waking up with him this morning, how gentle he was with me, how amazing it felt being with him. But then the other part of my brain reminds me that I don't even know him, that I let him get so in my head that I had a fight with Celia and Paige, that I almost lost my chance at an internship. My internship! The interview is tomorrow. And then what? I'm going to be going back home the next morning, and he's still going to be here.

It just . . . it isn't going to work out. He made me lose my focus. And I can't let that happen again.

*But he didn't make you lose your focus. He made you feel free.*

"I can't," I say. "I'm sorry, I just can't."

Abram pulls away and looks at me, studying my face for a long moment.

*Fight for me. Convince me, and I'll change my mind.*

But he doesn't. Instead, he takes his arms from around my waist and kisses me softly on the lips. Then he turns and disappears into the crowd, leaving me there to burst into tears.

Crying and being brokenhearted on a party cruise while your friends get drunk and dance with boys is definitely not my idea of a good time. In fact, it's kind of my idea of the worst time ever.

So I do the only thing I can do—I head for the bathroom and lock myself in a stall. There's a line of people waiting and a constant stream of girls coming in and out, but I don't care. There are enough stalls and enough turnover that I'm pretty sure I can stay in here for a while before anyone says anything.

At least, that's what I thought.

Until there's a quiet little knock on the door.

"Someone's in here," I snap. Don't they know that you're supposed to check for feet?

"Quinn?" a familiar voice asks.

I don't say anything.

"Quinn, it's Aven," the voice says. "Are you okay?"

"I'm fine," I reply firmly.

"Okay."

I can see her feet—she's wearing gladiator sandals, and her toes are painted a pretty peach color. They stay planted in place even though I just told her I was fine.

A second later, she tries again. "Are you sure?"

"Yeah," I say, realizing she's not going to give up without some kind of explanation. "I'm just a little seasick."

"Quinn," she says, sighing, "I saw you crying."

"I'm not crying!" Lie.

"You were when you came in here," she says, sounding confident. "I saw you."

"No, you didn't, because I wasn't crying." Lie, lie, lie. I have that weird feeling you get when you cry where your head is all heavy and your nose is all stuffed up. I give a sniff, because I can't help it.

"You're still crying!" Aven says. She starts pounding on the door. "I heard you sniff! Let me in!"

"No!" I say. "I'm going to the bathroom."

Her feet move away from the stall, and I let out a sigh of relief. But then her face appears underneath the door, peering up at me. "You are not going to the bathroom," she says. "And you don't seem seasick."

"Oh, for the love of god," I say, reaching out and unlocking the door.

Aven comes shuffling in.

If she thinks we're going to have some big bonding moment in here, she's definitely mistaken. "If you think we're going to have some big bonding moment in here, then I'm sorry to disappoint you, but I'm not in the mood."

She ignores my comment and looks at me. "Oh, Quinn," she says softly. She reaches over and grabs some toilet paper off the roll and hands it to me. "Blow your nose," she commands.

I do as I'm told, not because I want to, but because I kind of just want her to go away. Hopefully if I do what she says and I can convince her I'm okay, she'll leave me alone.

"Here," she says, reaching into her bag and pulling out one of those mini cans of Sprite. She pops the top and hands it to me. "Drink."

"I'm not drinking in a bathroom stall."

Aven rolls her eyes. "Knock it off, Quinn, it's not con-taminated."

Something about her insistence and the way she's hold-ing the soda out to me is actually kind of comforting, so I do what she says and have a drink. The soda is warm, and yet somehow still refreshing.

"Thanks," I say.

"Feel better?"

"Actually, I kind of do."

Aven nods in satisfaction, like she knew all it would take was some warm Sprite. She reaches for the can and takes a sip.

"So why are you hiding in the bathroom?" she asks.

"Why do you care?" I shoot back.

"Quinn . . . ," she starts, then takes a deep breath, like she's about to launch into some big speech about our friend-ship. My heart soars with hope for a second, wondering if she's going to say she's sorry for everything that happened, that she shouldn't have blown me off after Lyla got so mad at us. But then a look of doubt passes over her face, and I wonder if maybe she's actually going to tell me why we *can't* be friends anymore. And I can't take hearing that, not right after what just happened with Abram.

"Stop," I say. "I can't . . ."

She nods. "You want to talk about it?"

I shake my head, even though I *do* want to talk about it. The *real* it, not some dumb bullshit about not getting into Stanford or missing out on an internship. "It's a boy," I blurt.

"Oh." Aven nods in understanding, like she knows exactly what that's like. "He broke your heart?"

I shake my head, not sure if you can count what's going on with me and Abram as him breaking my heart. "I don't know," I say. "I just met him. And he seems . . . I mean, it seems like maybe he likes me."

"So then what's the problem?"

"The problem is that we're all wrong for each other. And he lives here. And I hardly know him."

Aven shrugs, like all this is totally normal. "The heart wants what it wants."

"Yeah, well, what if the heart is really messed up and confused?"

"All hearts are messed up and confused."

"So then how can I trust what's real and what isn't?"

She shakes her head. "You can't."

"You're making no sense." Seriously, she's talking in riddles. I should have known better than to confide in her.

There's a knock on the stall door. "Come on!" someone yells. "There are people waiting out here! Find somewhere else to do that lesbian shit."

Aven sighs and then stands up. She turns to go, and just when I've written her off as not knowing anything about love or anything else, she turns back around. "Quinn," she says seriously. "If you've found someone you really like, and he likes you back . . . well, that's amazing. He must be pretty special if he's making you react like this. And I know we're not friends anymore, and you don't know what's going on in my life. But you need to trust me when I tell you this—if you think you have a chance with someone you really like, well, then you need to follow your heart. That, I know."

She gives me a comforting little squeeze on my shoulder and then walks out of the stall.

Here is how the rest of the night goes (although there's really no need for a recap—if I ever wanted to remember it, all I would have to do is look in the dictionary under "predictable"):

Celia gets drunk and pukes over the side of the boat. Paige holds her hair back.

I don't see Abram again, which is actually kind of weird. I mean, we're on a boat—it's not like he could just disappear. Unless he jumped overboard and swam back to shore in an effort not to have to talk to me. (Ha-ha. Only half joking.)

When we get back to the hotel, Paige and I sneak Celia inside and down to their room, hoping no one sees us. Thankfully, no one does, except this really annoying girl named Juliana who shakes her head sadly at Celia, like *oh, drunk again*, when everyone knows Juliana's one of the biggest partiers in our school. But whatever.

Celia pukes again on her way into the room, all over the carpet in the hallway. But I'm not in the mood to deal with it, so after I make sure she's settled into her bed on her side so she doesn't vomit and choke on it in the night, I make Paige deal with the mess before heading up to my room.

I'm dreading seeing Aven after what happened in the bathroom, or Lyla after what happened on the beach—but luckily, I have the room to myself. I put my headphones in and download one of those apps that's supposed to hypnotize you into relaxing, but it doesn't help.

I can't stop thinking about Abram—the hurt look on his face tonight, the feel of his lips on mine, how he's a perfect mix of predictable and surprising. I wonder how I can like him so much when there are tons of guys at my school who are more my type that I couldn't care less about.

*Maybe those guys at school aren't really your type.*

The thought is jarring. *Of course* they're my type. They're smart and interesting and almost all of them have gotten into good schools.

*But maybe it matters more how you feel when you're around someone than what their GPA is or if they go to community college.*

But even if that's true, it doesn't have anything to do with me and Abram. He lives in Florida. And with any luck, I'm going away to Stanford next year. Everyone knows that long-distance relationships are doomed, especially when the guy is a superhot club promoter who's meeting new girls every night.

Besides, after today, I'm sure Abram wants nothing to do with me.

And it's this thought—knowing that he walked away from me tonight, that he didn't even try to convince me to stay—that's the final nail in the coffin of hope, the final roadblock that stops my heart in its tracks before it has a chance to take over.

# FOURTEEN

WHEN I WAKE UP THE NEXT MORNING, THERE'S a split second where my body is awake but my brain isn't quite there yet. It's a moment of sweet relief before the events of yesterday come rushing back to me. My mouth is dry and my head is heavy, even though I didn't drink last night. I glance at the clock. Eight a.m. Three hours until I have to be in downtown Siesta Key for my brunch interview with Biogene.

I glance around the room. Lyla's bed is empty. Aven's in bed, but she's always been a really heavy sleeper, so I won't have to worry about waking her up while I get ready.

I start the shower and let the water get hot while I send a quick text to Paige.

**Celia okay?**

I doubt they're going to be up this early, not after the night they had, but I know Celia will get pissy if she thinks

I didn't at least check in on her. Plus, if I'm being completely honest, I kind of don't really care if I wake Paige up. I have a flash of guilt as I remember how I left her last night, to clean up Celia's mess (literally and figuratively), but I don't feel *that* bad. There's been a lot of times I've been the one to have to clean up after Celia by myself, and a couple of times I've even had to clean up after the *two* of them by myself. So whatever.

Once I'm out of the shower, I dry my hair, then throw on shorts and a T-shirt. I pull out my laptop and spend the next hour or so brushing up on my Biogene facts and learning about the woman who's supposed to be interviewing me. Her name is Dya Brown, and she actually seems pretty interesting. She went to Stanford (yay!—something to bond over), and won a bunch of research awards while she was there. She graduated eight years ago, so she's young enough to hopefully remember what it was like to be in my position—about to finish high school and starting to plan my future.

After I've brushed up on my facts, I steam my interview suit, wishing I'd thought about the fact that I was going to be interviewing in Florida, and maybe brought something a little less heavy. The skirt part is fine, but the jacket seems a little formal for the Florida heat. Oh, well. It still looks really good on me (my mom believes in getting things tailored, even jeans, which I've always thought was crazy, especially since her tailor is this old Italian woman who's always trying to hook me up with one of her sons, but now I'm glad my mom's so on top of things), and that's all that counts.

As I'm sliding my feet into a pair of sensible black pumps, Paige texts me back.

She's feeling better! Gonna take a scuba-diving lesson, boat leaves at ten, won't be back until late—good luck at your interview, we know you're going to do greeeeatt xxo

I get annoyed for a second, thinking about how they're just taking off for the day without me. Why would they book a scuba lesson when they know I'm not going to be around? What am I supposed to do? Just spend all day by myself? They really can be pretty selfish.

But whatever. I can't think about that right now.

I have an interview to go to.

It's not that far from the hotel to the outdoor café where I'm supposed to meet Dya, and even though the sun is high in the sky, there's a nice breeze coming off the ocean, and it feels cooler than it did yesterday.

So I decide to walk, figuring I'm going to get there early anyway, so if I end up a little bit of a mess, I can just pop into the bathroom and fix myself up. As I walk, I get a text from my mom, listing all the things to remember to tell Dya, reminding me not-so-subtly that if I want to get into Stanford, it's important for me to get this internship.

I know she's right—Stanford's already rejected me, and even with my dad's connections and promises, I'm going to need all the help I can get.

Usually when my back is against the wall like this, I thrive. I've always done really well under pressure. But as I walk toward the cafe, even though I should be excited, all I feel is dread. My legs are heavy, my stomach is churning, and I can feel myself starting to sweat under my suit.

I try to tell myself I'm just nervous because I want this so badly. But I've been in situations where there's a lot riding on something, and I've never felt this way before. The sun feels blindingly hot, even though I know it's really not, and spots swim in front of my eyes.

I take a couple of deep breaths, and after a few more steps, I start to feel better. By the time I get to the café, I'm almost back to normal.

And then I see her.

Even though I'm early, she's already here. She's sitting at a table near the door, a glass of orange juice in front of her, tapping away on her iPad. I recognize her from her picture on the Biogene website, but she looks different at the same time. I know, of course, that everyone is going to look different from the pictures on their companies' websites, that those pictures are taken professionally so the company can look their best to prospective clients and employees.

But still. The woman in front of me looks like she's aged

a lot since her picture. She has dark circles under her eyes, and even though she's meticulously dressed in a white linen suit and black slingbacks, she looks too . . . I don't know, *formal*. Like the kind of person who's constantly having to worry about spilling something on themselves, or saying the wrong thing. It's not that she's nervous—it's actually the opposite of that. In fact, she looks like she's comfortable being like this, comfortable being so buttoned-up and in control.

My stomach does another flip as I take a step toward the café. I bypass the hostess stand and slip into the bathroom, deciding to give myself a quick once-over before my interview.

After being in the sun for so long, it takes my eyes a second to adjust to the darkness of the bathroom. I glance in the mirror. My face looks clammy and my forehead is shiny. I take a paper towel and mist it with the anti-shine spray I have in my purse, then pat it on my skin. I regloss my lips, adjust my suit, then gather my hair into a professional-looking loose bun.

*You got this,* I tell myself. *This is everything you've ever wanted, and you're going to nail it*. I check to make sure I have nothing stuck in my teeth, give myself what I hope is a confident smile, and then walk out into the restaurant.

I head immediately for Dya's table. She's on the phone now, and I can overhear her telling someone in a cheerful voice that she'll take care of it, but her face looks drawn.

When she sees me standing there, she ends her phone call. She gives me a friendly smile. "Quinn?" she asks, standing up and holding her hand out to me.

I freeze.

In the middle of the café, in front of Dya and everyone, I freeze. It's like my feet just refuse to move.

A look of confusion passes over Dya's face, like maybe she has the wrong girl, like maybe I'm not Quinn after all.

"Quinn?" she tries again.

The room starts to spin, and my vision blurs around the edges. I give Dya a smile and open my mouth to tell her yes, sorry, it's me, I'm Quinn, I'm happy to meet her and so excited to have this opportunity.

*Before graduation, I promise to . . . do something crazy.*

"I . . . ," I manage.

Dya frowns.

I open my mouth to try again.

But nothing comes out.

I turn around and run out of the restaurant.

I thought I'd start to panic once I was out on the sidewalk. I thought my throat would close up and my heart would flutter and my breathing would get shallow. But it's just the opposite. Now that I'm out in the fresh air, I actually feel better.

It's the same feeling I had the other day when I was on the boat with Abram, when I realized I didn't have to worry about getting good grades or playing by the rules.

I walk fast, wanting to put as much distance between myself and the café as I can. The last thing I want is Dya coming after me and asking me what's wrong. But after a few minutes it starts to become clear that's not going to happen, so I start to relax.

Holy crap! I just walked out of my interview with Biogene. If that wasn't doing something crazy, I don't know what is.

I wander down the street, stopping briefly to buy myself an iced latte and a blueberry-lemon tart from a corner bakery. I eat it and then continue my walk. Even though it's hotter now than it was when I left the hotel this morning, I don't feel flushed or uncomfortable.

All I feel is happy.

And free.

I wonder if I'm having some kind of mental breakdown. Or maybe it's one of those rebellious phases teenagers have sometimes, the ones where they do all the right things until they get to college, and then they start partying and going crazy because they finally have freedom. Of course, I'm not even in college yet, but still.

I'm shocked to realize I don't care what the reasons are, that I'm just happy I'm not sitting in that café on this beautiful day, interviewing for an internship I'm not sure I deserve.

It's like a high, deciding what you really want to do and then just doing it.

My phone rings, and I look down at the caller ID, expecting it to be someone from Biogene, asking me what the hell is going on.

But it's not.

It's my mom.

I expect to feel nervous, but I don't.

"Hello?" I say. It comes out sounding cheerful, even though I wasn't trying for that.

"Quinn?" my mom asks, sounding panicked. "Are you okay?"

"I'm fine," I say. "Did they call you?"

"Yes, they called me! Why did you run out like that? Are you sick?"

"Mom, I don't want to do the interview with Biogene."

There's silence on the other end of the line, and then my mom puts on her soothing doctor voice. "Quinn, honey, it's normal to have some anxiety about this, but you know that avoiding challenging situations won't make them any easier."

"I'm not anxious," I say, although I guess that's not completely true. I'm not anxious about the interview. But I *am* anxious about ending up doing something I don't want to do, or spending the rest of my time in Florida working for something I'm not even really sure I want anymore.

"Then what is it?" my mom demands, her distress at the thought of me ruining the family name apparently overriding her ability to sound calm and in control.

"I just . . . don't want the internship." There's no doubt in my voice while I'm saying it, even though there's just a tiny sliver of it in my mind. A tiny, tiny little voice that tells me I shouldn't be saying it. But that's only because it's a habit, like when you go to a restaurant and order the same thing every time. It feels uncomfortable because it's different, not because it's wrong.

"Quinn, that's ridiculous," my mom says. "Of course you want the internship. It's all you've ever wanted."

"No, that's . . . I thought I wanted it. But now I don't know what I want." I take a deep breath. "Mom, don't you think it's a little weird that it was *my* interview, and yet they called *you* to see if I was okay?"

"Of course they're going to call me, Quinn, I'm your mother! They were worried about you!"

"If they were worried about me, they would have followed me out of the café or called me directly! They called you because you're the one they're worried about, Mom. You're the one who has a connection to them."

"Quinn, I don't know what you're talking about, but whatever it is, we can discuss it later. Right now you have to go back to the café. The woman has agreed to wait there for ten more minutes, but if you're not back by then—"

"I'm not going back," I say. "I don't want the internship."

There's silence on the other end of the line, and it's a scary silence, the kind of scary silence that makes me realize my mom is really, really mad.

"Quinn," she says. "You will go back to that café. Now."

"No."

"Quinn," she says, like she thinks that starting sentences with my name is going to change my mind, "if you don't go back to the café, your father is going to be very, very upset with you."

"Why?" I challenge. "Because he wants me to have the internship? Or because he's worried about how you guys are going to look if I don't go back?"

Another scary silence.

"Mom," I say. "Please, you have to understand that I'm—"

But the line goes dead.

My mom hung up on me.

I stand there for a second in disbelief, just staring at the phone. My mom has *never* hung up on me before. Of course, I've never done something so blatantly against what she's wanted me to do.

That's the craziest thing about the whole situation—not that she hung up on me, but that this is the first time I can remember ever going against her wishes. Of course, until just now, I didn't realize I even wanted to go against her wishes.

*Abram.*

Suddenly, I have an overwhelming urge to see him, to talk to him, to explain why I stood him up. But how? I don't have his phone number, and it's not like I can just ask Celia for it.

Can I?

I type her a quick text.

**Can u give me Abram's number? I left something at his house.**

I stare at the screen before slowly deleting it. First, Celia might be crazy, but she's not stupid. She's going to know exactly why I'm asking for Abram's number, and she might try to talk me out of calling him. Not that it would work—but still, having to deal with Celia's questions (and inevitably, Paige's, since Celia would immediately tell Paige and then Paige would start texting me, too) sounds like a very unpleasant way to spend the morning.

*Just go over there. You're right near his house.*

The thought is deliciously exciting. And scary. What if he slams the door in my face, what if he doesn't want to see me, what if he yells at me and tells me to leave?

*What if he doesn't?*

These are the thoughts swirling through my mind until finally I find myself there, in front of his house, on a street that's foreign yet familiar, the street where Lyla and Beckett came to find me, the street where a neighbor called the police on me. (Well, not on me, exactly. But it sounds way more exciting when you put it that way.)

His car is in the driveway.

He must be home.

I don't hesitate.

I march up to the door and ring the bell, feeling brave and courageous and all the things you need to be when you're about to do something crazy like this.

But as soon as I see him, everything changes.

I don't feel brave.

I don't feel courageous.

I feel scared and nervous and worried he's going to take one look at me and send me home.

He's wearing a soft-looking gray T-shirt and his hair is messy and there's stubble on his chin and I want to kiss him so badly it's all I can do to keep from throwing myself across the porch and wrapping my arms around him.

For a split second, I see a look of genuine happiness cross his face, like he's glad I'm here, but then his face closes up and gets hard.

"Hey," I say, deciding to cling to that first look he gave me and not the closed-off look he's giving me now.

"What are you doing here?" he asks.

"I came to see you." I realize now I should have had a plan. I should have figured out what I was going to say, what

I was going to do to convince him I'm being honest, that I really do want to see him, that I care about him, that it makes no sense but that I want to get to know him better, to see if there could be anything between us.

"Why?" he asks.

"Because I missed you." The words come out of my mouth before I can stop them, and he sighs and then steps out onto the porch. He sits down on the top step and looks up at me.

"You missed me," he repeats.

"Yeah."

"That's why you're here?"

"Yes." I raise my chin into the air and give him a defiant look, daring him to contradict me.

"And you came to tell me this while wearing a business suit?"

"No." I shake my head and try to gather my thoughts, realizing that listening to your instincts has a risk—a risk that you might not know what to say in the moment, that you might not know how to tell the person in front of you that you really do miss him, that you can't stop thinking about him, that it's crazy and irresponsible and ridiculous, but the only thing you want right now is to be with him.

That old guilt resurfaces for a second, and I get angry at myself for thinking the most important thing in my life right now is a boy. A boy I just met. A boy I just met who's obviously mad at me, a boy I might never even see again after today. But then I realize it's not about Abram being more important than any of the goals I'd set for myself—instead it's about the things I *thought* I'd wanted not being important anymore.

"I had a job interview," I say. "Well, not a job interview. An interview for that internship."

"Oh. How did it go?"

He's still sitting on his porch steps, but he hasn't invited me to sit down next to him. And the way he's sitting, with his knees apart, taking up as much space as possible, makes me think he doesn't want me to.

"Not that great," I say.

"I'm sorry."

"No, don't be. I mean, it went horribly, but that's because I ran out of the restaurant before we had a chance to do the interview."

I expect him to ask me why, for me to tell him the story of how I saw that woman sitting there, how I saw my future flash before me, and how I didn't like it. How I knew in that moment I needed to follow my heart, that I had to do what felt right, and that's what led me here, to him.

But instead he just looks at me and says, "Why are you here, Quinn?"

"Because I wanted to see you."

"You already said that."

"Oh." *Tell him. Tell him how you feel.* "I guess . . . I mean, I guess I wanted to apologize. For standing you up."

"You didn't have to do that."

"I know, but I wanted to."

"Why?"

"Why?"

"Yeah, why did you want to apologize?"

"Because I'm sorry?" It's a confusing thing for him to ask. Why else would I want to apologize? People usually apologize when they're sorry for something.

"Yes, but *why*?" he presses.

"Because I shouldn't have done it. It was rude and mean and I . . . I didn't want to stand you up. I wanted to be with you, I wanted . . . I wanted to spend time with you last night."

"Then why didn't you?"

"Because I was scared."

"Of what?"

I think about the question, because I want to make sure that when I answer, I'm being completely honest. "I guess I was scared that I was losing myself. When my mom called and told me about this internship interview, I—I realized that I'd almost missed it because I was out on your boat. So I got scared."

"And you freaked out."

I nod.

"Just like you did today."

"What do you mean?"

"I mean you freaked out again today. Just a little while ago, at your interview."

I frown. "No."

"No, you didn't freak out today? Because you kind of just said that you did." He sighs and shifts his weight forward on the step, and something about the gesture sends panic flying through me. It's like he's about to stand up and walk back into his house, out of my life forever.

"No, I mean, I did freak out today. But it's different from what happened yesterday."

"How?"

"Because today I'm doing what I really want to do. I want to spend time with you, I want to be here."

"But why does it have to be one or the other? You could have spent time with me yesterday after you talked to your mom, you could have spent time with me today after you went to your interview. But you didn't. Instead, you stood me up, and you only came here *after* you decided you didn't want that internship."

"It's not that simple," I say, shaking my head because he's starting to make me confused. "Yesterday I stood you up because I got scared. I got scared that being with you made me too focused on you, that being with you might make me lose out on my dream."

"And yet here you are, less than twenty-four hours later,

telling me that isn't your dream after all, that you don't want that internship, that you're sorry you stood me up, but now you want to spend time with me." He shakes his head. "Quinn, I'm not going to be your distraction."

"You're not!"

"Really? Because it's a little weird that you somehow only end up being around me when the rest of your shit is falling through. When you think you don't have Stanford or your internship, that's when you want to spend time with me."

"No," I say, shaking my head. The feeling of panic is stronger now, because I feel like if I don't say the right thing, if I don't make him understand, I'm going to lose him forever. "That's not true."

"Really?" he says. "Because it sure seems that way."

"No, I don't . . . *I'm* the one who chose to leave the interview this morning. I decided I shouldn't put my energy into something I don't even want, that I'm going to stop wasting my time on things I only thought were important."

"Well, that's awesome," he says. "But every time you do something you really want, I become your excuse. And I'm not okay with that." He stands up. "I think you're really confused, Quinn. You need to figure out what you want, and I just . . . I wish you luck, but I'm not going to be a part of that. I really like you, and I just . . . I can't."

He looks at me, waiting for me to say something.

But I don't know what to say.

I miss my chance.

And after a second, he gets up and walks inside.

# FIFTEEN

WHEN I GET BACK TO THE HOTEL, I JUST WANT
to be by myself.

I want to throw myself down on my bed and cry. I'm
angry—angry at my mom, angry at myself, angry at Abram,
angry at Celia and Paige for going on some stupid scuba-
diving trip when I need them—but it's like I can't access that
anger. Instead, I'm just sad. Sad and tired.

When I open the door to my room, Aven and Lyla are
there. Lyla's sprawled out on her bed, and Aven's lying on her
cot, her hand over her head.

For a second I think about leaving, but then I realize I
have nowhere else to go. And besides, should I let them chase
me out of my room? If I want to lie here and be miserable,
then I can.

I throw myself down on my bed.

No one says anything for a while.

"Why are you guys just lying here?" I ask finally.

"I'm sad," Aven says.

"I'm wrecked," Lyla says.

"Life's a mess," Aven says.

"I want to go home," Lyla says.

"Me too," I say. "To all of the above."

I want to ask them what's wrong, why they're sad, why they're wrecked, why they want to go home, but it's really none of my business. Besides, if I ask them what's wrong, they might think they can ask *me* what's wrong, and then what will I say? That I slept with a guy and then when I confessed my feelings for him, he rejected me? It's completely humiliating.

And that's when my sadness melts away and the anger takes center stage.

"You know what?" I ask, propping myself up on my elbow and looking at Aven and Lyla. "This is ridiculous."

"What is?" Lyla asks.

"That we're in Florida, and we're just sitting in this room. We should be out having adventures." It's ludicrous, when you think about it. Our last day here, and we're just . . . sitting around! I mean, talk about an embarrassment.

"Sounds exhausting," Lyla says.

"Sounds depressing," Aven says.

I stand up and throw a pillow at Lyla. Then I throw another one at Aven. "Get up," I say. "We're going out."

Lyla looks at me like I'm totally crazy. "The three of us?"

she asks incredulously. *"Like, together?"*

I wait for her to tell me no, that she's not going anywhere with me and Aven. But for the first time since we had our fight, she doesn't sound totally opposed to the idea. And if I can play it right, she might just say yes. "Do you have anyone else to hang out with?" I challenge.

"No, but . . ." She trails off, like she's racking her brain for the million and one reasons it's a bad idea for the three of us to hang out.

"I'm in!" Aven says, jumping up off her cot.

"Me too," Lyla says, surprising everyone. She glances at herself in the mirror over the desk. "But can I wash my face first?"

"Of course," I tell her.

Aven and I wait in stilted silence while Lyla changes and washes her face. When she comes out of the bathroom, she grabs her purse. "Okay," she says. "I'm ready."

We all look at each other.

Suddenly, I'm regretting suggesting that the three of us hang out. Talk about a disaster waiting to happen. And after what just went down with Abram, can my heart withstand another disappointment? I'm really not sure.

But what can I do? It's too late now. I can't just call the whole thing off after I was the one who brought it up in the first place. How crazy would that be? They'd know. They'd know I still cared so much, that I still missed them so much, that the only reason I haven't reached out to them, that the only reason I pretend I don't care is because I care so, so, so much.

But I can't say that.

Even if it's true.

In the elevator on the way downstairs, we come up with rules for the day. No talking about our fight. No talking about the emails we sent to ourselves. Aven comes up with that last one, and it's confusing to me at first. Why can't we talk about the emails we sent? It makes me wonder if her email maybe has something to do with why she's so upset, if she did something her email told her to and then ended up regretting it.

"This might be awkward," Lyla says when we get to the sidewalk outside the hotel.

"Not any more awkward than sleeping in the same room," I say, which isn't really true. Sleeping in the same room is way less awkward than this. First of all, sleeping is just sleeping. And second of all, now we're going to be forced to interact. To talk. To hang out. Can we really go all day, or even a few hours, without bringing up the past?

We head down to the beach and wander around for a while, collecting shells until our pockets are overflowing. It's a good way to start things—we don't have to talk much, and we can even wander away from each other as we walk on the shore.

We stop at the farmers' market and buy cute little blue bottles to pour our shells into, then top the shells with sand from the beach. It's the perfect souvenir, and it doesn't escape me that every time I look at it, it's going to remind me of Aven and Lyla.

As we leave the farmers' market, Aven and Lyla are talking about how the three of us used to buy the exact same things all the time, but I'm too distracted to focus on what they're saying. I can't stop thinking about Abram. He's never far from my mind, and every time I see anyone who's the same height as him or even remotely fits his description, I start to panic, thinking it's him.

"You wanna get lunch?" I ask Aven and Lyla once we're back on Ocean Boulevard. The last thing I want is to end up with nothing to do. I'm barely hanging on to my sanity as it is.

"Sure," Lyla says, and I breathe a sigh of relief.

We stop at the first restaurant we see and choose a table outside. I try to just enjoy the gorgeous weather and not think about Abram. But it's impossible. It's like he's imprinted on my brain.

When the waitress comes over to take our order, we decide to just get a bunch of appetizers to share.

"No sour cream on the fish tacos," I say automatically,

because Lyla hates sour cream. I glance at her. "Right?"

She nods.

"Can you believe this?" Aven asks. "Did you ever think we'd end up sitting here together at the end of this trip?"

"No," I say. There were a lot of crazy things that happened on this trip—not getting into Stanford, losing my virginity . . . honestly, the fact that I'm sitting here with Lyla and Aven is probably the least crazy thing that's happened to me so far.

Aven takes a deep breath and fiddles with the straw in her drink. "I know we're not supposed to be talking about the past, and you don't have to give me any details, but . . . did you guys do what your emails said to?"

I look away, waiting for one of them to answer before I do. I don't want to be the first to admit I was crazy enough to actually put stock in an email I sent myself when I was fourteen.

For a second, no one says anything.

I'm not above lying—if they say they haven't done what their emails told them to, then I'll say I didn't, either.

"Yes," Lyla says, looking right at me and raising her eyebrows, like she's expecting me to be the only one who didn't follow through.

"Yes," I say, looking at her in defiance, daring her to be shocked.

"Yes," Aven says.

Silence settles over the table, and there's a moment, an opportunity for one of us to speak up and tell the others what happened, what we did in order to fulfill the promises we made to ourselves four years ago. I study Lyla's and Aven's faces as they both shift on their chairs uncomfortably, and I wonder again if somehow the emails are the reason we're all sitting here together. I mean, it's our senior trip. Something must have gone horribly wrong for the two of them to not have any plans or anyone to hang out with today. I know it has for me.

But none of us are ready to go there—we made a rule not to talk about those emails, and even if we hadn't, opening up about them seems too vulnerable. It's one thing to be out here, eating lunch together, it's another to start talking about the intimate details of our lives. Especially when my life is kind of—okay, totally—a mess right now.

So instead we make small talk about the trip and gossip about our classmates as we work our way through the appetizers. When the waitress asks us about dessert, we order a cookie-dough sundae to share.

I marvel at the fact that we're sitting here, talking to each other, getting along after all this time. I don't want it to end.

"We should do it again," I blurt before I can stop myself or think about the consequences of what I'm saying.

"Do what again?" Lyla asks.

"We should make more promises. Why not? We're at the beach." The last time we wrote those emails to ourselves, we were at the beach. And the fact that we're here again seems almost like a sign. And yes, doing what my email told me to do was a complete disaster, but isn't that the point? That I should give myself another chance, a do-over?

For a second, Lyla and Aven look like they're about to laugh, like maybe they think I'm joking or something. But when they see I'm serious, they get quiet, thinking about it.

"Sure," Lyla says after a second. "I'm in."

Aven nods. "Me too."

Later we walk down to the beach, and once we're there I hesitate, my purple marker poised over the sheet of light-green paper Aven picked out at the souvenir shop.

We decided to write our promises down on real paper this time instead of sending emails. I wonder if it's because some part of us doesn't want to have the emails showing up four years from now, blasting us in the face, reminding us of what we want to accomplish, forcing us to do things that might end up making things worse.

Or maybe it's just because we're starting to realize that when you make a promise to yourself, there's no deadline. That you have to work on it every day, that our lives are a work in progress, that it really is all about the journey.

One sentence.

That's what we promised each other.

And this time, we're not going to put a time limit on it.

*I promise to . . .*

I want it to be something important.

Something I should be working on for the rest of my life.

*I promise to . . . learn to be happy.*

When we're all done writing, I fold my piece of paper in half.

"Ready?" I ask, holding out the Siesta Key, Number One Beach lighter we picked up at the gift shop.

We all nod. I hesitate for a moment, wondering if we should read our promises out loud, the way we did last time. But then I realize that's not what this is about—last time, our promises were promises to each other as much as ourselves. And this time, whatever we've written on those papers is ours and ours alone.

I watch as the papers go up in flames, flying into the air and disappearing before the ashes drop into the ocean.

The three of us stay there for a while, sitting on the sand and watching the sun dip below the horizon. We don't say much. We don't have to.

I know we're all thinking the same thing—there won't be an email this time to remind us of the promises we made. We're going to have to remind ourselves.

# SIXTEEN

THAT NIGHT, I HAVE A HARD TIME FALLING ASLEEP.

I keep thinking about Abram.

How it felt kissing him.

How he moved slowly on top of me, looking into my eyes, brushing my hair back from my face.

How he held my hand while we walked over the tricky part of the wall toward the cove.

How even though he's lived here his whole life, he made everything seem new and interesting.

How hurt he looked when he realized I'd stood him up.

How upset he seemed when I came to his house to tell him I was sorry.

How I felt when he sent me on my way.

How it feels to know that I'm leaving soon, and I'll never get another chance to talk to him. I don't even have his phone number. And even if I did, he made it perfectly clear that he doesn't want to see me again.

I finally fall into a fitful sleep, and when I wake up the next morning, I'm in a really bad mood. I end up taking it out on Lyla and Aven. I know it's not fair, but even so, I can't stop myself. I accuse them of taking my hair straightener, which is ridiculous, since I know they didn't, and even if they had, I wouldn't have cared.

I head down to the lobby early, just wanting to get this whole trip done and over with.

Celia and Paige are already down there, looking relaxed and fresh in matching strapless chevron maxi-dresses. They both have two tiny braids woven into their hair with colorful beads on the end.

"There you are!" Celia says, like I'm the one who ditched them yesterday and not the other way around. "We've been looking for you."

"Really?" I ask, still grumpy. "Because you didn't text me or anything."

Paige sighs. "Are you mad about yesterday?" She turns to Celia. "See? I told you she'd be mad about yesterday."

"You are?" Celia asks, taking a delicate sip of the iced coffee she's holding. "You're mad we went on a scuba trip?"

"No," I lie. "Where'd you guys get the beads?"

"Oh, the boat stopped at the other side of the key, you know, so people could get out and walk around. It was like a mini cruise or something! There was a little stand selling these dresses for ten dollars! And you could get your hair done for ten more!" Celia does a twirl, showing off, not caring that maybe I'm not going to be so psyched that the two of them are wearing matching dresses and matching hair beads and apparently had a fun day while I was having a complete breakdown.

"How was your interview?" Paige asks me, as she plays on her phone.

"Great," I lie. "Thanks for asking."

By the time we board the buses for the airport, I feel like strangling both of them. I know they're not really doing anything wrong—it's just the mood I'm in.

When we get to the airport, I order a coffee and dump four sugars into it, hoping the jolt of caffeine and sugar will help me feel better. I sit in the boarding area with Celia and Paige, wondering what's going to happen when I get home, what it's going to be like to have to admit to my mom that I don't want to go to Stanford anymore, that I don't know *what* I want, exactly.

My stomach churns the whole flight, but by the time I board the bus that's going to take us back to school, I'm actually feeling very Zen about the whole thing. Is my not going to Stanford the worst thing that could happen? My mom will get over it. Right?

As we pull into the traffic circle in front of school, I wonder for a second if maybe she's not going to be there to pick me up, even though I reminded her about a million times that I was going to need a ride home. (We weren't allowed to drive ourselves—we needed a parent or guardian to pick us up, because we couldn't leave our cars parked at the school for so long.)

As Mr. Beals and a couple of the boys from our class start unloading our suitcases and lining them up on the pavement, I run my eyes over the crowd of cars for my mom's navy-blue Lexus.

I finally spot it, but I'm not close enough to see her face through the windows, to get a read on what kind of mood she's in.

I grab my suitcase and turn around to head for the traffic circle.

And that's when I come face-to-face with the most gorgeous eyes I've ever seen.

"Hi," Abram says, giving me that smile, the same one he gave me on the beach the very first day I met him, the same one he gave me at the cove while we were eating breakfast, the same one he gave me when he announced he'd invented a fold-up boat.

"What are you doing here?" I blurt. My heart is beating fast and my face feels flushed, and I don't know what he's doing here, but I'm glad he's here and I can't believe it.

"I came to see you," he says, like it's totally normal for him to be here instead of in Florida. "I mean, I . . . I went to your hotel, and you weren't there, so I got on the very next flight to Connecticut, and I just . . . I found your Facebook page, and then I found out what school you went to, and I . . . I don't know, I came here." He looks sheepish, like he realizes this plan is crazy, even for him.

"But *why*?" I ask.

"I missed you." He says it so simply and honestly that I melt.

"I missed you, too."

He looks around. "Is there a place we can go to talk?"

"Yeah," I say. "Yeah, there is."

He nods. "I can bring you home after." He holds up a set of car keys. "I have a rental."

"Okay," I say, trying to stay calm. Butterflies swarm my stomach and goose bumps break out on my arms. Abram is here. He followed me all the way to Connecticut! He came here just to see me! "Just give me one second."

The cars in the circle are moving at a leisurely pace toward the pickup area, and I make my way through the line and over to my mom's Lexus.

I knock on the window.

She rolls it down.

I can tell as soon as I see her face that it's not good.

Her mouth is set in a tight line. "Get in," she says.

I shake my head. "No."

"No?" She sounds as shocked as I feel.

"I'm not . . . I have a ride home."

"You have a ride home? With who? Celia?"

"No. With Abram."

"Abram? Who the hell is Abram?" She shakes her head and doesn't wait for an answer. "It doesn't matter. Quinn, get in the car. We'll talk about this at home."

"No, Mom." I take a deep breath. "Yes, I want to talk about this. But I'm not going home with you. And I'm not going to Stanford."

She opens her mouth to reply, but I cut her off.

"Even if Dad can somehow figure out how to get me in, I'm not going. I don't want to." As I'm saying the words, I realize just how true they are. I don't want to go to Stanford if I have to bribe my way in. All I'd be thinking about while I was there was how I didn't deserve it, how I'd only gotten in because of my dad.

It's weird, but for those hours where I thought I'd been rejected and there was nothing I could do about it, I'd had some of the happiest times of my life. Yes, some of that had to do with Abram. But some of it had to do with me, and with finally doing what I'd actually wanted to, and not what I'd always *thought* I'd wanted.

And yes, part of me still felt sad when I realized I wouldn't be living in Palo Alto next year—but I wasn't sure if that was just my brain creating emotions based on habits instead of what I really wanted. I wasn't exactly *sure* what I really wanted—but I needed to start making new connections and figuring it out. Maybe it was Yale. Maybe it was Georgetown. Maybe it was the University of Miami, or maybe it wasn't college at all.

"Quinn, you're being ridiculous," my mom says. "Please, get in the car."

"No." I shake my head. "Mom, I love you. And I do want to talk about this more. But not right now. Right now I have something to take care of."

And before she can say anything else, before she can convince me not to do it, I run back across the traffic circle to where Abram is waiting.

"Everything okay?" he asks, his eyes flicking over to where my mom's car is now stuck, waiting behind a white Toyota Highlander.

"Yes," I say, as a feeling of calm and peace washes over me. "Everything's perfect."

Abram's rental car is nice—a black Chrysler 300 with leather seats.

"So where to?" he asks as we buckle our seat belts.

I'm about to direct him to a café nearby, so we can grab a coffee and talk, but then I stop. "No," I say, shaking my head.

"No?"

"No."

He looks confused. "No what?"

"No, I don't want to go anywhere with you."

"Oh." He swallows. "Okay. I know it's a little weird, me just showing up here like this. I'm sorry if I made you uncomfortable." I see the disappointment on his face, and I realize he thinks I mean I don't want to see him at all, that I'm not glad he came. Which is so far from the truth I almost laugh.

"No, I mean, I don't want to go to a coffee shop or to get something to eat. I want to talk first. Right here, before we go anywhere."

"Oh." Abram breathes a sigh of relief. "Okay."

"Why did you come here?"

He reaches over and fiddles with the heater. "Because I wanted to see you."

"But you basically told me yesterday you didn't want anything to do with me."

He tilts his head and looks at me, then avoids the question. "Are you freaked out that I'm here?"

"No." I shake my head. "I'm happy you came."

"You are?"

"Yes."

He reaches down and unbuckles his seat belt, then turns so he's facing me. "Look, I know it's a weird situation, I know it's . . . yeah, I know it's crazy. I've only known you a couple of days. But when you left yesterday, Quinn, I couldn't stop thinking about you. I tried to get you out of my mind, I tried to tell myself you were just a girl passing through and I should forget about you. But I couldn't."

My heart is pounding and my face is hot and my stomach has so many butterflies I'm afraid they're going to come bursting through my skin. "I couldn't stop thinking about you, either," I say. "But what about all that stuff you said? About me needing to figure things out, about you just being a distraction?"

He reaches for my hand, his fingers making little circles on my palm, each touch sending fire blazing through my skin. "I still think you have a lot to figure out," he says. "But I . . . I want to figure it out with you."

His hand goes down to my seat belt, and he unbuckles it and pulls me close. His eyes stay on mine, just like they did that night, the night he held me and moved inside of me and made me feel like everything was perfect and right. "I want to figure it out with you, too," I say. And I know it's crazy and he lives far away and I don't know him that well, but there's a connection, right here, right now, almost crackling with its intensity, and as his lips meet mine, this moment is all that matters.

We're about to go get something to eat when my phone buzzes with a text.

Hey, it's Aven—I'm locked in the bathroom by the gym,

can you please come and help me out?

I stare at my phone incredulously. What is she talking about? Locked in the bathroom by the gym? How the hell did that happen? Well, if she thinks I'm going to postpone hanging out with Abram so I can go rescue her from her stupidity, she's got another thing coming.

I look around the parking lot toward the front of the school, searching for Mr. Beals or another teacher I can send in to help her. But there's no one. Abram and I have spent so much time out here talking and kissing, that everyone else has cleared out and gone home.

I think about texting Aven back and telling her I already left, but that would be really mean. And yeah, it's probably her own fault that she locked herself in the bathroom, but still. I can't just leave her there—what if something bad happens?

"I'm sorry," I say to Abram. "I'll be right back. My friend is having an emergency."

"Sure," Abram says. "Everything okay?"

"Oh, yeah," I say. "It'll only take a minute."

A second after I get to the gym, Lyla turns the corner, coming from the other hallway, the one by the office.

"Hey," I say.

"Hi." She looks confused. "Are you . . . did Aven send you a text, too?"

"Yeah, about being locked in the bathroom?"

We look at each other, and I can tell we're both thinking the same thing—doesn't Aven have any other friends to text? And why did she need two of us to come and rescue her?

"Whatever," I say, and push on the bathroom door. To my surprise, it opens right away. Maybe it was locked from the inside? Lyla follows me in, but it doesn't seem like anyone's here.

"Aven?" Lyla tries.

There's no answer, and for the first time, I start to really worry. What if something happened to Aven? What if she's in a stall somewhere, passed out or hurt? Lyla starts opening the stall doors, and I follow suit, starting at the opposite end.

But before we can finish, the door to the bathroom opens and Aven walks in.

"Aven!" I say. "Why the hell did you tell us you were locked in the bathroom?" I mean, seriously. If she was locked in and someone let her out, she should have at least sent us a courtesy text, letting us know she was okay.

"Yeah," Lyla says accusingly. "I was worried about you."

But Aven doesn't say anything. She just turns around and locks the door behind her.

"What the hell are you *doing*?" I ask. Is Aven crazy? It wasn't enough that she got locked in the bathroom, now she wants us *all* to be locked in here? I try to push by her and out the door, but it's no use. It's locked.

Aven puts the key back into her pocket. How the hell does she have a key to the gym bathroom anyway? And why is she locking us in here?

"I'm sick of this," Aven says. "I'm sick of not being friends. I'm ready to make up." She takes in a deep breath. "And none of us are leaving this bathroom until we do."

TURN THE PAGE FOR A
SNEAK PEEK AT AVEN'S STORY:

LAUREN BARNHOLDT

Author of *Two-way Street*

FROM
THIS
MOMENT

THE MOMENT OF TRUTH BOOK 3

I LOOK UP.

There he is.

Liam.

My best friend.

The boy I've been in love with for four years.

He walks easily across the parking lot, his black back-pack slung over his shoulder, his hair slightly messy, a coffee in one hand. He looks up and spots me and Izzy standing there, and he gives us a wave.

I marvel at how easy he's walking, as if he doesn't have a care in the world. That's always been so strange to me—how one person can have been my whole entire world for the past four years, how his every action, his every word has affected me on such a profound level. The things he's said can either knock me into the stratosphere of happiness, or throw me into the depths of despair.

How can he not know how I feel? How is it that I've been so good at hiding the thing that's been the biggest part of my life for all these years?

"Hey," he says when he sees us. "How are my two favorite girls?"

"Good," I say.

"Great," Izzy says.

She smiles up at him as he leans down and gives her a kiss.

Which is another huge reason that after this weekend nothing will ever be the same. Because after this weekend, my best friend is going to know I'm in love with her boyfriend.

# JOIN THE
# Epic Reads
## COMMUNITY

## THE ULTIMATE YA DESTINATION

### ◀ DISCOVER ▶
your next favorite read

### ◀ FIND ▶
new authors to love

### ◀ WIN ▶
free books

### ◀ SHARE ▶
infographics, playlists, quizzes, and more

### ◀ WATCH ▶
the latest videos

### ◀ TUNE IN ▶
to Tea Time with Team Epic Reads